ECHOES OF THE HEART

TETON MOUNTAIN SERIES
BOOK 2

KELLIE COATES GILBERT

Copyright © 2024 by Kellie Coates Gilbert

All rights reserved.

No part of this book may be reproduced in any form or by any electronic or mechanical means, including information storage and retrieval systems, without written permission from the author, except for the use of brief quotations in a book review.

Cover Design: Kim Killion/The Killion Group

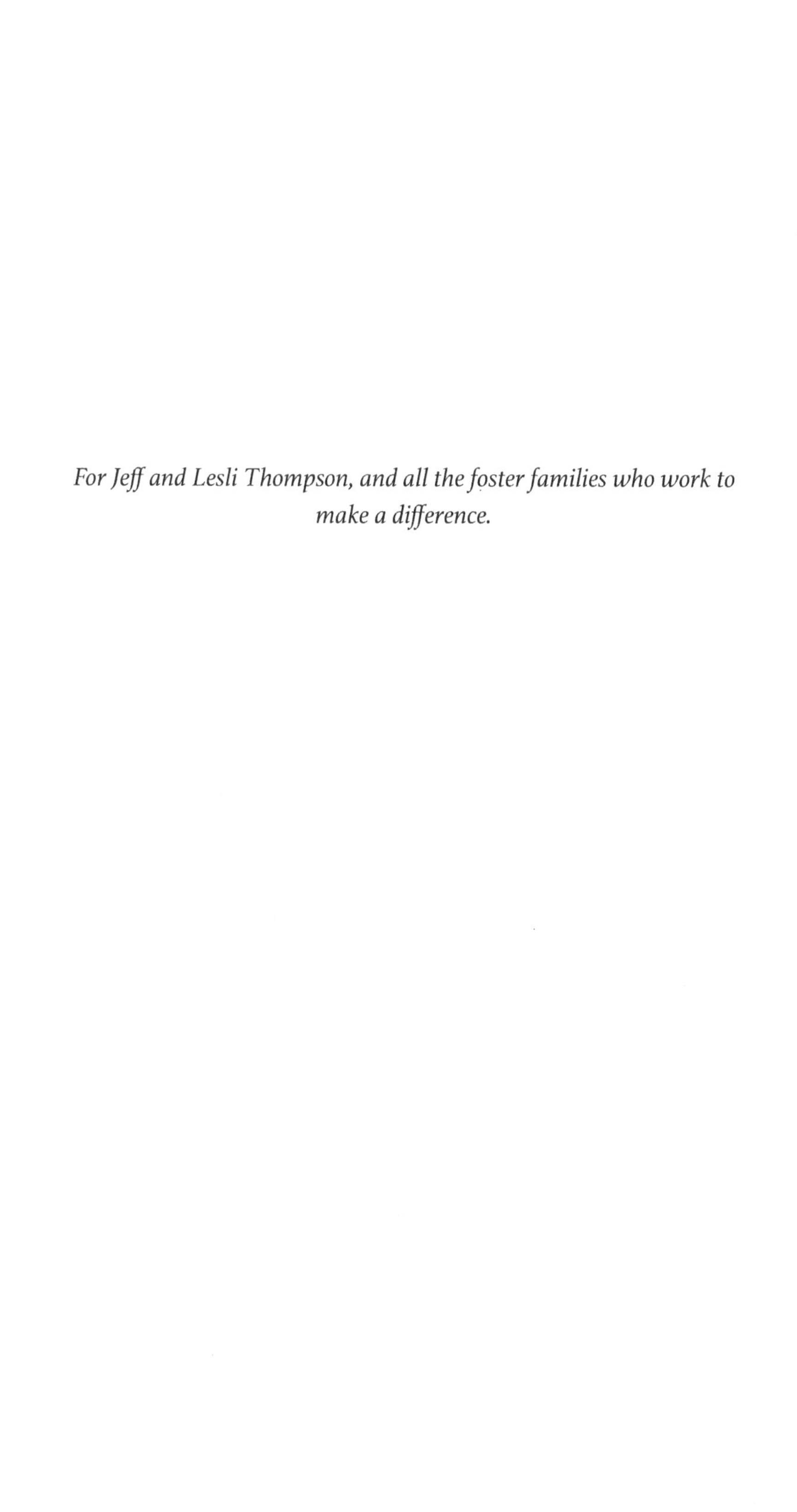

For Jeff and Lesli Thompson, and all the foster families who work to make a difference.

PRAISE FOR KELLIE COATES GILBERT NOVELS

"If you're looking for a new author to read, you can't go wrong with Kellie Coates Gilbert."
~**Lisa Wingate**, NY Times bestselling author of *Before We Were Yours*

"Well-drawn, sympathetic characters and graceful language."
~**Library Journal**

"Deft, crisp storytelling" ~**RT Book Reviews**

"I devoured the book in one sitting." ~**Chick Lit Central**

"Gilbert's heartfelt fiction is always a pleasure to read."
~**Buzzing About Books**

"Kellie Coates Gilbert delivers emotionally gripping plots and authentic characters." ~**Life Is Story**

"I laughed, I cried, I wanted to throw my book against the wall, but I couldn't quit reading." ~**Amazon reader**

PRAISE FOR KELLIE COATES GILBERT NOVELS

"If you're looking for a new author to read, you can't go wrong with Kellie Coates Gilbert."
~**Lisa Wingate**, NY Times bestselling author of *Before We Were Yours*

"Well-drawn, sympathetic characters and graceful language."
~**Library Journal**

"Deft, crisp storytelling" ~**RT Book Reviews**

"I devoured the book in one sitting." ~**Chick Lit Central**

"Gilbert's heartfelt fiction is always a pleasure to read."
~**Buzzing About Books**

"Kellie Coates Gilbert delivers emotionally gripping plots and authentic characters." ~**Life Is Story**

"I laughed, I cried, I wanted to throw my book against the wall, but I couldn't quit reading." ~**Amazon reader**

"I have read other books I had a hard time putting down, but this story totally captivated me." ~**Goodreads reader**

"I became somewhat depressed when the story actually ended. I wanted more." ~**Barnes and Noble reader**

ECHOES OF THE HEART

TETON MOUNTAIN SERIES, BOOK 2

Kellie Coates Gilbert

1

"Pull!"

As the clay pigeon launched into the air, Reva Nygard tracked the bright orange disk with laser focus. Her finger tightened on the trigger, and with a resounding bang, she shattered the target. The crowd erupted in applause.

Capri Jacobs, one of her best friends from high school, stood nearby, a grin on her face. "Way to show 'em what you're made of."

Reva's face displayed every bit of her delight. "Thanks, Capri," she replied, reloading her shotgun with ease.

The scent of freshly fired gunpowder hung in the air as Reva stepped back up to the shooting station at the Thunder Mountain gun range, her boots sinking slightly into the soft ground as she found her stance. Her long black hair dangled in a braid down her back as she nodded, the cool confidence she often exuded in the courtroom now directed toward the blue horizon.

A second clay pigeon shot into the air. Reva tracked it with unerring focus, her trigger finger curling around metal. Time seemed to slow as she followed the orange disk's trajectory, and then, with fluid grace, she shot.

A deafening bang resonated through the valley as the shotgun unleashed its payload. Reva's target disintegrated into a cloud of orange dust, the remnants scattering like stardust against the vibrant backdrop of the Teton Mountains.

The townspeople gathered at the event cheered. A fellow shooter and the town veterinarian, Tillman Strode, shook his head. "Great shot, Reva," he said, admiration in his voice.

Reva's heart swelled with pride, her keen senses soaking in the scent of pine needles and damp earth mixed with the heady aroma of chili cooking. In the distance, Oma Griffith, Betty Dunning, and Dorothy Vaughn—known as the Knit Wits to everyone in Thunder Mountain—waved their spoons and ladles in a show of solidarity before returning to dishing up bowls and handing them out.

Competition was stiff here at the annual skeet shoot and chili cook-off. Not only were the best local marksmen lined up to compete, but some serious cooks were standing over simmering pots guarding their secret ingredients. The funds raised would go to charity. This year's money would help remodel the community center, a place where both seniors and youth could gather.

"I think you've got this," Capri leaned and lowered her voice, cupping her mouth with her hand. "Doc Tillman is your only real rival, and he seems to be losing his focus. You've got him doubting himself."

"You think so?" Reva whispered back. She rarely let her proclivity for conquering her opponents take backstage—even when there seemed to be so little at stake.

Reva's affinity for victory was undeniable. Winning was simply in her DNA, a reflection of her unwavering determination and unrelenting pursuit of excellence.

She'd once been accused of not knowing how to relax.

Perhaps true, but she loved giving life one hundred percent every waking hour. Especially now when her efforts served the residents of her beloved Thunder Mountain. As mayor, she could think of no better focus than on her neighbors and friends.

The final round came down to the wire, with Reva managing to maintain her lead.

As that last clay pigeon disintegrated in the air, she knew she had done it. She could easily win this competition, impressing the crowd, and herself as well. She'd already pulled off a personal best, shooting forty-seven out of fifty—a feat anyone would be proud of. Now, only one more to go to complete victory.

The sun began to dip in the sky and the mountains perched as silhouettes against the fading sunlight. A hushed anticipation settled over the attendees as the organizers gathered at the makeshift podium, where a gleaming trophy awaited its rightful owner.

Reva, her heart pounding with exhilaration, stood alongside the other competitors, including Doc Tillman. Capri waved from the crowd, beaming with pride. The scent of victory was palpable. She rarely missed a shot in all her years of competing.

Reva squinted under the bright sky, her finger resting lightly on the trigger. Out of the corner of her eye, she caught sight of Doc Tillman's hopeful eyes. The clay pigeon launched, a fleeting target against the vast blue.

With a gentle sigh, she subtly adjusted her aim. The shot rang out, echoing her decision across the field. The orange disk sailed away unscathed, and a surprised cheer erupted for the beloved veterinarian.

Albie Barton, the newspaper editor, served as the tournament announcer. He cleared his throat and raised the award high. "Ladies and gentlemen, we have a winner," he declared, his voice carrying across the range. "With an incredible display of marksmanship, our very own Doc Tillman has claimed the title of the Thunder Mountain skeet shooting champion!"

Everyone burst into cheers and applause, clapping their hands and whistling in appreciation. Reva's cheeks flushed with the warmth of their admiration for a man who deserved every bit of the honor. She couldn't help but smile as he accepted the shiny trophy, shaped like a stylized clay pigeon in mid-flight.

Doc Tillman held the prize close, his eyes glistening with a mix of gratitude and accomplishment. "Thank you, everyone," he exclaimed. "This means the world to me."

"Congratulations, Reva!" Capri whispered as she threw her arms around her friend in a tight hug. "You did it!"

Reva scowled. "What are you talking about?"

Capri grinned. "You have a sneaky habit of stepping aside to let others pass you."

She shrugged and smiled back. "People who take the high road encounter less traffic."

Capri squeezed Reva's shoulders. "Let's get us a bowl of chili, then we'll head out to Teton Trails and celebrate the news of your non-win with Lila and Charlie Grace." Capri held up her phone. "I've been texting with them. Lila is at the ranch helping Charlie Grace birth that calf that's giving her trouble."

The two women linked arms and approached the tables lined with simmering pots of chili, the spicy aromas mingling in the air. "Well, what have we here?" Reva said, stopping in front of the Knit Wit ladies.

Oma Griffith immediately scooped a sample of their entry into a disposable paper bowl and handed it to Reva with a spoon. "We know you like chocolate and—"

Betty Dunning gave her a sharp elbow jab. "Shh...that's our secret ingredient."

Dorothy Vaughn rolled her eyes. "Well, not now, it isn't."

Oma's expression immediately filled with horror. "I—I didn't mean to—"

Reva leaned close. "No worries. Your secret is safe with the mayor."

Capri failed to suppress a chuckle despite covering her mouth with her hand. "Uh, with me too. I won't tell."

The promise seemed to bring some relief to the ladies across the table.

"So, what do you think?" Dorothy urged.

Reva tasted the chili and gave an appreciative groan. "Oh, it's delicious."

As the mayor, she understood the weight of her impartiality, the importance of each smile and nod as she sampled the contestants' heartfelt efforts. With spoon in hand, she moved from one entry to the next, her taste buds alighting with flavors both bold and subtle. Her words were measured, her praises genuine but evenly distributed, ensuring no hint of favoritism clouded the spirited competition. In each spoonful, she tasted not just the ingredients but the love and pride of her community.

As the day's celebrations continued around her, Reva reflected on her love for Thunder Mountain. From her unexpected role as the town's mayor to her newfound passion for skeet shooting, Thunder Mountain had embraced her, and she had embraced the town in return.

Upon graduating from high school, she'd left Thunder Mountain to pursue a prestigious education at Tulane University, after which the allure of high-powered law firms in New York, Chicago, and Los Angeles beckoned her with promises of success, wealth, and prestige. She could have had it all, but she chose to return to this small, tight-knit community in Wyoming, and she never looked back.

In Reva's mind, success was not solely defined by external recognition or a hefty bank account. True accomplishment was about making a difference in the lives of the people you cared about and being a part of something greater than yourself.

Thunder Mountain meant more to her than just the picturesque backdrop found on postcards in Dorothy Vaughn's Bear Country Gift Store. It was the heart of her existence, a place where her roots ran deep. She'd grown up in this mountain town and three of her best school friends had remained close. They were her tribe.

Charlie Grace was a single mom who owned and operated the Teton Trails Guest Ranch, an enterprise she opened just last spring. After a rocky start, the ranch was now thriving—as was her relationship with both her father and her new guy friend, Nick Thatcher.

Lila and her teenage daughter lived at the other end of town. Like Charlie Grace, she was raising a daughter on her own. Six months into her pregnancy, her husband of less than a year tragically died in a helicopter crash in Fallujah.

Lila currently worked with Doc Tillman down at the veterinary clinic, which was perfect given her love of anything soft and furry. Despite all that she juggled, Lila returned to school via an online program from the University of Colorado to pursue a large animal veterinarian license with a specialty in horses. "Camille's college fund needs a bit of help," she claimed. "I need the money the extra certification will provide." Never mind the fact that she was nearly killing herself in the process.

Capri Jacobs still lived with her parents. When questioned about the decision, she shrugged. "It's free." The rest of them knew full well that cash did not weigh in as the deciding factor. Capri owned Grand Teton Whitewater Adventures. She killed it financially, especially during the heavy tourist season. Her chosen profession also left her available in the winters when she alternated filling her time with binging seasons of *Gilmore Girls* on television and snowmobile racing on the local circuit.

Wild adventures aside, Capri dedicated herself to taking care of her mother and stepdad, a man who thankfully traded in his affinity for bourbon and replaced it with lemonade several years back. Sadly, Dick now fought a cancer diagnosis.

Reva's girlfriends had become the pillars of her life, the steady constants, especially after her split with Merritt. No matter what else demanded their attention, they gathered weekly over drinks and dinner, sharing their joys and struggles. As the years passed and she never married or had a family of her own, their importance grew even more profound. These girls were her air. Without them, she wouldn't be able to breathe.

Sure, there were moments of loneliness that crept in, most often when she saw families thriving. A deep place in her heart that longed to be a wife and mother was a companion she couldn't quite outgrow.

"So, what do you say? You want to head out to the ranch and share the news with Charlie Grace and Lila?" Capri asked, her voice breaking into Reva's mental reverie.

Reva looped arms with her close friend. There was no reason to tarnish her day with melancholy. Instead, she'd focus on how her life was richly blessed with the love and camaraderie of these extraordinary women, and so much more. Like they said in her weekly meetings, gratitude helps you fall in love with the life you already have.

"Good plan," she said, grinning. "I can't think of anyone I'd rather celebrate my tournament loss with."

2

The night held a whisper of chill as Reva's car headlights cut a swathe through the darkness blanketing the winding gravel road. She pressed the toe of her teal-colored Lucchese boots against the brake pedal as she approached the intersection ahead. After coming to a complete stop, she looked both ways before easing her black Escalade onto the highway that would lead to her home.

Okay, sure. There wasn't another pair of headlights anywhere near, but she was a rule follower. How would it look if the mayor broke the law?

Reva leaned and turned on the radio, pressing on the compact screen until her favorite station blared. Immediately, a Carole King song she adored filled the inside of her car. She opened her mouth and sang about feeling the earth move under her feet—loud and slightly off-key.

What did it matter? No one would hear her fail to hit the proper notes.

Outside the car window, the moon cast a gentle glow over the looming peaks of the Teton Mountain range that stood as a sentinel around the valley. As she drove, her mind drifted back to the evening with her girlfriends. Despite years of knowing them, there were still surprises.

Upon arrival, she and Capri stepped inside the barn, the earthy scent of hay mingling with the musky odor of manure, a pungent reminder of the rawness of life on a ranch. The straw beneath her feet had felt uneven and scratchy against her new boots.

"You afraid you'll wreck those spendy things?" Capri teased as they made their way across the hard hay-packed floor to where an anxious Charlie Grace stood over Lila, who was bent down in the straw.

"You hush," Reva told her. "I've about had enough of you tonight." In a playful gesture, she shoulder-bumped her friend.

Lila yanked the black rubber glove off her right hand and squirted orange-colored disinfectant all over her fingers and palm, then up her arm. A resolute look filled her face as she placed the remaining gloved hand against the belly of the cow lying on its side. The poor thing bellowed as apparent pain shot through her body.

Reva's eyes widened. "Oh, my goodness."

Charlie Grace scowled in her direction. "Shh...let Lila concentrate."

"Help me," Lila instructed, motioning to her sleeves. "We've got a calf that's breech."

Without need for further instruction, Charlie Grace bent by her friend's side and rolled the fabric up above Lila's elbows.

"A little more," Lila told her.

Reva and Capri exchanged worried glances as Charlie Grace complied.

Lila's expression was now a mask of fierce determination as she faced the cow. "Ready, girl?" With her arm, she swiped perspiration from her brow.

The cow, large and anxious, mooed lowly as Lila's full arm disappeared inside, searching, feeling for the calf's hind legs.

The tension was palpable, the air thick with anticipation and worry.

Reva had watched, her stomach churning, as Lila's facial muscles tensed, her jaw set in concentration. The visceral, almost invasive nature of the act was both awe-inspiring and deeply unsettling. The sounds of Lila's grunts, the cow's distressed moos, and the squelching, wet noises of her arm maneuvering inside the animal painted a scene of raw, primal urgency.

Then, with a final, determined pull, Lila guided the calf's legs into position. The cow pushed, and the calf slid into the world, hind legs first, coated in fluids and the stark, undeniable evidence of life's messy entrance.

The calf lay there for a moment, steaming in the cool air of the barn before taking its first shaky breath. It was a moment of profound relief and triumph, nature's ordeal culminating in the miracle of life.

Reva exited the highway and drove down the lane to her house.

Despite the discomfort and the gore, she couldn't help but feel a surge of wonder and respect for the unyielding force of nature and Lila's unflinching effort. Still, a fresh notion hit. Perhaps she wasn't as anxious to give birth as she'd earlier thought.

As she pulled into her driveway, Reva was welcomed by her two-story log home with its soft lights shining through the windows.

Her house, built on the banks of the Snake River, was a showcase of mountain chic décor. While relatively simple in terms of form, she'd paid a lot of attention to luxurious details. Warm tones, local stone and timbers, inlays of metals, and lots of leather furnishings created an inviting interior. Soaring open-beamed ceilings and walls of floor-to-ceiling windows married her home and nature.

Inside, the quiet was palpable—comforting, yet isolating. She moved through her nightly routine almost mechanically, her mind elsewhere. The bathroom sink's faucet emitted a steady stream as she brushed her teeth. Finished, she spit into the sink and rinsed.

In the soft, unforgiving light of her bathroom mirror, she traced the lines etched at the corners of her eyes and mouth. Each crease was subtle proof that her wrinkles grew more pronounced with every year. Wrinkles no expensive cream would stop.

She sighed, a mix of resignation and defiance mingling as she studied the evidence of time's relentless march. What would it be next? Creaking knees? Bifocals?

Reva unwrapped the ties on her plush robe and kicked off her furry slippers. The bed welcomed her with cool sheets that gradually warmed to her presence. Her ruminations, however, refused to quiet.

Images of the day's events unwound. The skeet shoot and the look on Doc Tillman's face as he examined hers, searching for evidence that she'd purposefully missed the clay pigeon. She was nothing if not a great actress. She was a master at hiding her true feelings—a skill that had landed her in regular AA meetings.

She turned her thoughts to the funds raised and the plans for the community center. She'd be meeting with the architects soon and laying out plans to build what she hoped would become Thunder Mountain's gathering place.

Well, that and the Rustic Pine. Nothing could replace Tom and Annie Cumberland's bar and grill, where locals celebrated victories, soothed defeats, and marked the milestones of life against a backdrop of clinking glasses and hearty laughter.

The echoes of those joyful noises seemed to linger in her mind as the memories of the day's warmth and revelry slowly drifted away, giving way to the quiet of the night. Reva yawned, fatigue from the day's emotions finally catching up with her. She nestled deep under her down comforter, letting the gentle pull of sleep claim her.

A SHARP POUNDING at the door downstairs jolted Reva from the depths of slumber. The loud, insistent knocking cut through the stillness of the night like a bolt sending her heart leaping and pulling her abruptly into startled consciousness.

Heart hammering against her chest, she reached for the Glock on her bedside table—a necessity for a single woman deep in the woods. The lights flickered on, casting her room in stark relief as she approached the window, her robe now clutched tightly around her.

Who could it be at this hour?

Her mind raced with possibilities, some more unsettling than others.

Peeking through the curtains, her breath caught. A figure from a past she'd considered closed.

He stood on the deck looking up at her, his features half-hidden in the shadows.

She raced down the stairs, stubbing her toe on the corner of the landing as she hurried for the door. She stood and reached for the knob, barely able to breathe.

"Reva, it's me. Let me in."

She creaked open the door letting a sliver of moonlight fall across her bare feet.

"Merritt? What are you doing here?"

3

Merritt looked up at her, his face a sonnet of suffering, lines etched deep not from age but from some unspoken weight. "I'm in trouble," he told her, his voice breaking as he said it.

Reva's breath caught. "Are you all right?" Her eyes scanned his torso for signs of injury. "Are you sick?"

He shook his head, dispelling the notion. "No."

"Is it Hillary? The kids?"

Again, he shook his head.

Reva filled with confusion. "Then, what are you doing here?" The last time she'd seen Merritt Hardwick was the night they'd said goodbye forever—or so she'd thought.

Merritt rubbed the back of his head. He wore a turtleneck sweater and jeans and still looked...good. Standing near him sent a tiny quiver through her. "Come in," she told him, wrapping her arms around her to ward off the chilly night air.

He obliged and followed her inside. Reva tightened her robe's belt around her waist suddenly aware she had no makeup on and must look a sight. Her hand went involuntarily to her hair.

The motion brought a tiny smile to his lips, a smile that faded as quickly as it appeared.

She let her eyes roam her ex-fiancé, examining every feature in the light. Despite their seven-year separation, he hadn't changed. He had the same lean build with muscles in all the right places. His warm, brown complexion, flawless. His hair was still shaved displaying his perfectly shaped head. And he still had those amazing dimples that gave him a boyish charm few women could resist.

She'd seen a few pictures of him over the past seven years. The media was generous the night he won his senate seat. He'd looked fabulous standing there waving at the cameras. So had his new wife, Hillary.

Reva felt her heart beat a little faster as their gazes met. Those familiar espresso-colored eyes flecked with gold cracked open her chest. All the years of knowing him—of him knowing her—rushed back. She froze in place hoping that by standing still she could stop the world from spinning.

She swallowed and tried to find her voice. "Please, sit." She motioned for the sofa. "Would you like something to drink?"

Merritt appeared awkward as he made his way to the sofa and sank into a cushion. "Coffee…unless it's too much trouble."

"No. I'll make some." She could use a cup as well. Normally the caffeine would hinder her ability to sleep, but she knew better than to believe she was going to get any more rest tonight.

Reva padded into her vaulted kitchen and busied herself with stuffing a paper filter inside her Breville coffee maker.

"You still drink that coffee from the roastery in Columbia?" he asked, making uncomfortable small talk as he glanced around.

She almost hated to admit she did. "Yes."

Her answer seemed to please him. "Good. That's good."

The drip coffee maker took forever. When the brew was

finally ready, she carried two steaming mugs back into the living room. She handed one to Merritt and cautiously took a seat opposite him. "Now, do you want to tell me why you just showed up on my doorstep in the middle of the night?"

He took a sip, taking forever to answer her pointed question. Finally, he directed his gaze back at her. "I'm in trouble."

She looked at him over her mug. "You said that. Do you care to explain?"

His attention drifted to the night sky outside her windows. "I've done something awful." His voice dropped an octave as he added, "And I got caught."

The revelation was like a spear in her heart. "What do you mean awful?" She held her mind back from racing through all the possibilities. Had he been unfaithful to Hillary? That would explain a lot.

"It's not what you're thinking," he said, establishing that he could still read her mind. He set his mug on the coffee table and leaned over his knees, his hands trembling as he knitted his fingers to steady them.

He was scaring her. She placed her mug on the nearby table. "Merritt, what did you do?" Her voice was nearly a whisper.

"The details don't matter. In fact, the less you know, the better. But, it's serious," Merritt started, his voice a mixture of defeat and regret. "I've just learned that for months now, I've been under a secret FBI investigation. They're looking into my connections with a foreign diplomat from Egypt. It appears they have evidence that I accepted significant sums in exchange for political favors."

Reva's hand flew to her chest. "Oh, my God." She closed her eyes tightening them against the revelation.

Merritt's hands were now shaking uncontrollably. "They're alleging that I violated the Foreign Corrupt Practices Act and potentially committed acts of treason. I'm likely to be charged with bribery, misuse of office, and breaching national security protocols." His eyes, once confident and piercing, now held a shadow of the man he used to be. "The funds were masked as donations to my campaign. In truth, they were direct payments influencing legislative decisions."

Reva leapt from her seat. "Merritt! No!" Unbidden moisture flooded her eyes as she paced the floor. "That isn't you." She turned to face him. "This is a joke, right?"

Tears streamed down his cheeks. "I was blinded by ambition, Reva. And now, everything I've built is on the verge of collapsing." His voice trailed off as he looked away, the gravity of his choices and the impending consequences settling heavy in the room.

Reva knotted her fist and brought it to her mouth, biting the skin as if the pain might mask the agony she felt inside.

Merritt met Reva's questioning gaze, her turmoil swirling like a storm. "I came to you because, despite everything, you know me better than anyone else," he confessed, his voice thick with emotion. "You were there at the start of my dream, believing in me, pushing me to follow my political aspirations." His voice dropped. "Despite what it cost you."

He wiped his eyes with the back of his broad hand. "I couldn't bear the thought of you finding out from the news and not from me." His gaze returned to his hands that were clasped tightly together. "I needed you to hear it directly from me, to know the truth behind the headlines that will soon break. I'm not seeking forgiveness from anyone, Reva. I don't deserve that. But before the world judges me, I wanted someone who knew the man I once aspired to be to understand the depth of my regret. You're my best friend...you deserve that much."

His words hung heavy in the air, a witness to the gravity of his revelation and the remnants of a bond that had meant everything. The notion did not pass that he'd called her his best friend. Present tense.

"What about Hillary?"

Merritt rubbed his forehead. "She left me."

"Left you? And the kids?"

"They are all at her parents' house in New Jersey. She's agreed to appear when I make my public statement, but it's over. She left no doubt of that."

"Oh, Merritt. I'm so sorry. About it all." She still couldn't reconcile the news with who she knew him to be. How could he have gone so off course? She couldn't bear to think about what lay ahead for him.

She looked into his eyes, hating the despair she saw there. She'd once carried that look. There was a time long ago when she was so ashamed of her drinking that she could barely hold her head up.

Is that why he came to her? Did he know she would understand?

Still, there was no excuse for what he'd done. And from the sounds of things, he was going to pay dearly.

The knowledge broke her.

She moved to the spot before him and folded to the floor, took his hands into her own. "Listen to me, Merritt. You are not the sum of the crimes you committed. You are better than that. You are deeply valued by your creator...and by me. Nothing changes that." She squeezed his fingers tightly with her own. "You will get through this. And when you are on the other side, you'll find a way to compensate for your poor choices. Make things right. Your bad decisions can be redeemed."

She longed to trace his chin with her finger, assure him he would never lose her friendship. Nothing could remove how she felt about him...continued to feel about him despite their moving on from each other.

As if reading her thoughts, he squeezed back. "I'm not staying in Thunder Mountain. I would never do that to you."

She nodded. "You're married," she whispered.

"Yes."

If everything was different, they might stay up until dawn talking about old times. Times they had made each other blissfully happy, and they'd laugh about the times they made each other blisteringly mad. They'd reminisce their love story like two people reflecting on a movie, their memories slightly different now, tinged with bittersweetness.

Things were not different. Their story came to an early and sad end. He'd moved away to follow his dreams and had married Hillary, had a family.

He was no longer hers.

She was not his.

The thought hit her hard. Their love was like a faded map, the once-bold lines and vibrant paths now blurred and indistinct. Each crease and tear a testament to a destination never reached. The landmarks that once seemed so familiar now appeared foreign, as if the very landscape of their deep affection had shifted, leaving behind only a relic of the past—a guide to a place she could no longer find.

She lifted. "Look, I'm going to go get the guest room ready. You'll stay the night."

She held her hand up to his immediate protest. "We both know there's no hotel open this late. Not unless you drive clear to Jackson Hole, and even then—" She let her voice drift off. "You'll stay here."

This time, he didn't argue. He simply stood. "Thank you, Reva."

He took his watch off, the one his grandfather had given him upon passing the bar exam, and laid it on the coffee table next to his mug. She knew it was engraved. *"I'm expecting big things. Love, Pappy."*

Thankfully, he was not here to see Merritt's tumble from grace.

Minutes later, they ascended the stairs, each step seeming

to creak under the weight of Merritt's revelation. The hallway light cast long shadows, stretching their forms into ghostly silhouettes that merged.

At the top, they paused, standing side by side, facing their separate doors. The space between them was charged with what remained unsaid. They exchanged a glance, a silent conversation of regret and resignation, a mutual acknowledgment of the boundary they dared not cross.

"So, if you get cold, the thermostat is on the wall next to the door." She pointed in that direction.

He nodded. "Thanks."

With soft, bittersweet smiles, they whispered their goodnights.

Merritt turned to his door, hand resting on the knob for a moment too long while she lingered, her gaze tracing the familiar lines of his back, memorizing the moment.

As their doors closed softly, the quiet of Reva's room enveloped her like a shroud, the echo of their footsteps a testament to what might have been and the poignant acceptance of what was.

4

Reva barely slept. Just before dawn, sheer exhaustion finally took over and she dozed, slipping into a deep, yet fitful, slumber and woke with a start with sunlight beaming through her window.

Immediately remembering the previous night's surprise visit, she bolted up and threw back the covers. "What time is it?" she murmured out loud, searching on the nightstand for her watch. "Oh, my goodness!" It was nearly seven a.m.

She scrambled from the bed. Without bothering to put on her slippers, she quickly crossed to the window and peered out.

His car was still there.

Her breath caught and her mind raced wondering if he was awake, or like her, had he fallen asleep. They didn't quit talking until nearly four in the morning.

It didn't matter. Right now, she needed to focus.

She tore off her bathrobe and donned a pair of jeans and a cute blue sweater. In the bathroom, she ran a brush through her hair and pulled it back into a pony, then washed her face and brushed her teeth before racing down the stairs. Thank-

fully, Merritt had always claimed she looked beautiful without makeup.

As soon as the thought entered her mind, she chased it away. She had no business trying to be attractive to her ex-fiancé. Especially now.

Merritt was sitting on her deck, looking out over the river, with a cup of coffee in hand. She got a cup and joined him.

"Hey," she said as she folded into the neighboring Adirondack. "I'm sorry I slept late."

Merritt gave her a weak smile. "Daybreak isn't exactly late. Besides, I'm the one who should be apologizing."

Reva let his statement hang in the air. She gazed out at the water tumbling over the riverbed, letting the sight steady her. "Did you sleep okay?"

"No," he admitted. The sallow look under his eyes confirmed his statement. He leaned over his knees gripping his mug. "I suppose you need to get to work."

"It's Saturday. But—"

He straightened. "I need to go. I don't want anyone to find out I'm here." There was worry in his voice.

Still, Reva found she wasn't quite ready to bid him goodbye. She'd missed him terribly. Missed how they used to be able to talk about anything and everything. Missed how they didn't need small talk. Missed how he could read her moods and knew just what to say, and when to remain quiet.

He knew her like no one else. Time did not erase that.

Unbidden tears stung her eyes, and Reva angrily blinked them away. Their story had been written long ago. A story that did not have the happy ending she'd hoped for. Last night he'd shown up with an epilogue that made everything worse.

She suddenly felt uncomfortable and completely out of her element. "Okay, then," she said, quietly.

Reva had secretly played this scene, or a similar one, in her mind a thousand times—especially in the early years after their split. Whole conversations had played out in her imagination.

Never did she doubt her decision not to follow him, but in her pretend world, he changed his mind and stayed. He chose her over his career. Never mind that he would have grown to resent her for giving up his dream.

About year five, the pretense had begun to fade. Lately, she'd rarely thought of Merritt or the new life he'd built for himself. She never allowed herself to check the internet for photos of his wife and children. Why continue to put herself through that pain?

Hillary had the man—and the life—she had so badly wanted.

Reva had so much to be thankful for. Yet, in her forties, she was still single with no family of her own.

"Are you okay?" Merritt asked.

She mentally cursed the fact he could still read her so easily. "No," she admitted.

A few moments of silence hung in the air.

Reva cleared her throat. "I'm sad. Deeply sad, Merritt. None of this is how I wanted things to be."

He placed his mug on the deck beside his foot. "I know. I feel the same. It's hard not to consider what might have been." His voice cracked as he struggled to continue. "I regret it." Then, looking at her, he added, "All of it."

He stood and turned to face her. Taking her hand, he removed her mug and placed it on the side table. Then he gathered her other hand in his and brought them both to his lips. He kissed her knuckles lightly.

Immediately, her anxiety faded away. Merritt Hardwick had that effect on her. Something in her spirit remembered she was safe in his presence.

Reva reluctantly pulled her hands back. "Are you hungry? I can fix you something before you go."

He quickly shook his head. "No, I need to get on the road. My plane is waiting at the airport, and I don't want to risk the media picking up on the fact I'm here. News hasn't broken yet, but it will. Likely within hours."

His reality sobered her. "Are you going to be all right?"

It was a stupid question. Of course, he wasn't going to be okay. He faced a humiliating disclosure of what he'd done, followed by lengthy legal negotiations that would no doubt end in prison time.

With luck, he would serve his sentence in a facility like where they'd sent Bernie Madoff and Martha Stewart. Federal white-collar criminals, and especially politicians, often served their time in what was termed Club Fed facilities, minimum-security establishments with low violence and amenities that rivaled many hotels. Still, he would be incarcerated, and the life he'd known would vanish along with his political aspirations.

His finger went to her cheek. "You know me. I'll be fine. I'll have the best legal team."

True. His father was wealthy and would fund his defense. While Merritt's political career was over, he'd step out of the prison walls into a cushy corporate job on the board of one of his dad's many enterprises.

His eyes had never looked more captivating. She touched his arm. "I'll be praying."

"I know you will." He knit his fingers with hers and guided her back into the house and out to his waiting car.

"Well, I guess this is it," he said, using the exact phrase he'd said seven years ago when he prepared to depart for D.C.

She nodded. "Yes, another goodbye." She tried to smile and found it painful. "It was good seeing you—even under these circumstances." She squeezed his hand before releasing it.

Merritt reached for the car door handle, then suddenly turned. His eyes filled with desperation. “Reva, you were a wonderful person to love. It felt good to love you—and to be loved by you. I just want you to know that.”

Melancholy filled her. She gave him a tender smile. “It was the easiest thing I ever did.”

5

Lila Bellamy tossed the empty Rice-A-Roni box into the garbage and returned to the stove where she stirred the pot on the burner. "Camille," she called out. "Dinner's ready."

Exhausted, she pulled plates from the cupboard and set the table. "Camille, dinner. Don't make me call you again!"

"Gosh, Mom. You don't have to yell." Her daughter slugged into the kitchen, flip-flops slapping the tiled floor.

Lila surveyed the girl dressed in baggy sweats and a T-shirt, hair pulled back. She wiped her hands on a kitchen towel. "Is that what you wore to school today?"

Camille shrugged. "Yeah." She scowled at her mother's inspection. "What?"

Lila sighed. "Nothing. Dinner's ready."

Her daughter padded over to the stove and peeked into the pot. "I'm on a low-carb diet."

Lila refrained from rolling her eyes. Last month it was twelve-hour fasting. Before that, the Mediterranean Diet and the Flexitarian eating program. Camille flitted between weight-loss programs like butterflies on mountain lupines. Besides, her petite blonde daughter didn't need to lose a single pound. She was already perfect.

Still, she knew better than to fight Camille about her eating habits. It wasn't worth the conflict. For the most part, she still ate healthy. "Fine. What do you want?"

"I'll just grab something on the way to the game," she said. "Do you have a twenty?"

"I'm not a bank," she reminded her daughter, even as she went for her purse.

Camille grabbed the bill from her mother's hand. "Thanks, Mom!" Despite her earlier pronouncement, she picked up the spoon on the counter, scooped rice from the pot, and slid it inside her mouth. Immediately, she grimaced. "Ew, how can you eat that stuff?"

Lila watched her daughter head back to her room. "Oh, Mom?" she called over her shoulder. "Can you drop me off at the game on your way to Reva's?"

Lila groaned. She'd forgotten this was their get-together night. After the long night out at Charlie Grace's the evening before, she'd planned on finishing up some online homework, then a hot bath and bed. Especially since she'd spent most of the afternoon dealing with car trouble.

"Baby, you're going to have to catch a ride. Did you forget my vehicle is in the shop?"

She could hear her daughter groan from down the hall. "That car is so lame."

Lila couldn't argue the fact, but she didn't have a choice. A new purchase wasn't in the budget. Camille needed several hundred dollars for volleyball camp, her own vet school tuition was due for next semester, and now this big expense. It never ended.

She'd received military survivor benefits after Aaron was killed but raising a daughter on a single income still had its challenges.

Lila pulled her phone from her jeans pocket. She should text her girlfriends. They'd understand if she bagged out.

Before she could tap out her message, her phone rang. It was Capri.

"Hey," her friend said when Lila answered. "I just heard your car is in the shop. What happened?"

"Ernie thinks I blew a gasket."

"Oh, no!"

Lila sighed. "Yeah, worst timing."

"I could look at it," Capri offered. "But if it is a gasket, the car might not be worth fixing."

Capri had an enviable mechanical ability. She could fix almost anything.

"Nah," Lila told her. "I'll figure it out. But I think I need to skip tonight—"

"No way. No skipping our girlfriend night. Besides, sounds like you need some fun."

Lila didn't want to argue. "Okay. But I'll need a ride."

"You got it," Capri promised.

Lila hung up and put the Rice-A-Roni in a plastic container, stored it in the fridge, and headed upstairs for a quick shower.

The sun was dropping behind the mountain peaks, its rays casting a soft, golden light through the pine trees as Capri pulled her car to a stop in Reva's driveway. "I hate to admit how much I'm looking forward to tonight."

Lila nodded. "Yeah, I'm glad you talked me out of changing my plans and staying home." She followed Capri inside.

"There you are." Reva motioned them to the kitchen island where Charlie Grace cradled a glass of wine in hand. Soft music played in the background. "You're late," she chided, her voice a mix of amusement and warmth.

Reva's affinity for punctuality was so legendary that people teased saying even the town clock outside city hall, in a silent act of respect, seemed to check itself whenever she passed by.

Charlie Grace pointed to the plate in front of her. "Aunt Mo made us some of her famous chocolate chip cookies."

Capri lit up. "Ooh...nothing goes with red wine better than chocolate."

Reva lifted her frosted mug and grinned. "Or, in my case, root beer."

Capri lifted a cookie from the plate and turned to Charlie Grace. "How's the new calf?"

"It was touch and go in those early hours. But the little heifer is now thriving. All thanks to Lila."

Lila uncorked a second bottle of wine, a Chablis that was one of her favorites. "Doc Tillman wasn't exactly happy I didn't call him to help."

Charlie Grace broke a cookie in half and frowned. "Why?"

Lila shrugged. "Technically, I don't have the certification yet. But the real reason? I think Doc Tillman feels a little threatened."

Reva gazed in disbelief. "Threatened. Why?"

Lila poured the wine with a steady hand. "Lately, I feel like every time I introduce a new technique or a fresh idea, there's this...vibe. Don't get me wrong, Doc Tillman has been amazing to learn from. He took a chance on me, and I'm grateful. We've worked together for years, but it's like he's not ready to acknowledge that times are changing. I really want to bring in some of the new stuff I've learned in the online program I'm taking at the University of Colorado—you know, to make a difference in the practice and streamline the office. But there's this unspoken tension lately. It's like walking on eggshells!" She recorked the bottle. "I respect him so much, but I can't help but push for progress. It's a weird mix of admiration and this undercurrent of, I don't know, competition? Anyway, it's complicated." She sighed and took a sip of her wine.

Reva picked up the plate of cookies and motioned for the girls to follow her into the living room. "Goodness, Lila. That sounds so tricky. But you know, it's amazing how you're handling the situation. You're bringing in new ideas, and that's important. Maybe Doc Tillman just needs time to adjust to the changes. Keep doing your thing, girl."

Capri, always the spirited one, chimed in with a grin. "Oh, come on, Lila—shake things up! You're there to make a difference, right? Don't let old traditions hold you back. I say, go for it!"

Charlie Grace, thoughtful as always, added, "I agree with both Reva and Capri, Lila. It's a delicate balance, but I think you're the right person to bridge the gap. You have a way of being respectful yet assertive. You've got this!" She eased onto the sofa, the plush cushions enveloping her.

Lila took a place beside her, taking care not to spill any wine as she plopped down. "Yeah, well...Doc Tillman likes to do everything by the book."

"Nonsense," Charlie Grace argued. "I can cite plenty of times he's found—uh, creative—ways to administer animal husbandry."

Capri grinned and turned to Reva. "Speaking of Doc Tillman. He has no reason to be cranky. He has *your* trophy."

Reva's hand went to her chest in mock astonishment. "Why, what are you talking about?"

"You know exactly what I'm referring to." She turned to the others. "Reva threw the annual skeet contest and let Doc win."

"Yeah, we know," Charlie Grace announced.

Reva whipped her head around. "You know? How?"

Charlie Grace shrugged. "The Knit Wits told Fleet Southcott who told Brewster Findley who told Nicola Cavendish." She paused. "And once it got to her—well, it was all over but the newspaper article."

Reva groaned. "Does Doc know?"

Lila twirled the wine in her goblet. "My bet is no. He was on the phone to Albie this morning making sure there would be an article in the next issue of the *Thunder Mountain Gazette* announcing his win." She turned to place her glass on the table. Her brows drew together as she reached for a watch and held it up to the light. "What's this?"

Capri glanced at the watch, then at Reva, her eyebrows raised in playful suspicion. "Is that a man's watch?" The corners of her lips lifted in a tiny smile. "Girl! You got a man in your house?"

Charlie Grace laughed. "Hey, are you holding out on us?"

Reva bolted from where she sat with her hand out. "Uh, can I have that?"

Lila turned the watch over, read the inscription, and frowned. "Oh, Reva."

"What?" the other two said nearly in unison.

Lila handed the watch to Reva who quickly pocketed the timepiece.

"Okay, yes. It's Merritt's watch," Reva admitted. "Not that it's anyone's business."

Charlie Grace's mouth dropped open in shock. "Merritt Hardwick? He was here?"

Lila scowled. "I didn't know you were still in touch."

Reva held up an open palm in protest. "Okay, look. We aren't in touch—well, not really. Not in the sense you mean."

"How do you mean?" Charlie Grace asked, also frowning.

"I haven't seen him since we split." Reva drained her root beer and set the empty mug on the coffee table. "But he showed up last night out of the blue. I was sound asleep when I heard pounding on the door."

Capri tossed a partially eaten cookie back onto the plate. "What do you mean? He just showed up here?"

"In the middle of the night?" Charlie Grace lifted her eyebrows. "That's a little nervy." It was common knowledge Charlie Grace was not a huge fan of Merritt Hardwick, not after he moved away and broke their friend's heart.

Reva nodded. "Yes, I don't disagree. Everything you say is true. He's...well, he's in trouble." She swallowed. "And he wanted me to know before news broke." She waved her hands staving off the inquisition she knew was coming. "But that's all I can disclose right now."

"I don't think you have to worry about betraying any confidence." Capri held up her phone. "Breaking news."

Reva jumped up and grabbed the remote for her television. She pointed toward the large screen mounted on the far wall. With one click, the screen brightened and immediately, Merritt's face filled the screen with a voiceover.

"In breaking news, Senator Merritt Hardwick was arrested hours ago after a lengthy FBI investigation into violations of the Foreign Corrupt Practices Act. The freshman senator is being charged with bribery, misuse of office, and breaching national security protocols."

The image on the screen immediately turned to footage of Merritt's arrest and *perp walk* as law enforcement officials handcuffed him and led him to a waiting car.

Reva shut the television off, tears pooling.

The others rushed to her side, offering any comfort they could.

"Oh, Reva. I'm so sorry," Charlie Grace told her, pulling her dear friend into a hug.

Lila followed suit. "You must be devastated. I mean, I know you're no longer together, but he still meant something to you." Lila knew what it was like to be haunted by memories of a love you no longer could count on. She'd also been the one who silently sat with Reva for several evenings after Merritt packed and left for Washington, D.C.

Capri was the only one to voice what everyone was thinking. "What in the world? Is he an idiot? It's a given Merritt's going to lose his political career for good. But he's also going to land his butt in prison. I mean, rocks for brains...right?" She looked between Charlie Grace and Lila for confirmation.

Charlie Grace scowled at her. "Uh, maybe a little sensitivity?"

Capri shrugged. "Yeah, okay. But I'm just saying..."

Lila led Reva back to the sofa and sat down beside her. "So, spill. What does this mean? Why was he compelled to show up in the middle of the night? You've not been a couple for years."

Capri's eyebrows lifted in suspicion. "Things haven't changed, right?"

Charlie Grace followed with a firm, "He's married."

Reva sighed. "Of course, I know he's married. Nothing has changed between us. Our relationship is firmly in the past. I'm just saddened, that's all. I still care deeply for him and wish him all the best. This? I don't understand it. Merritt's choices simply do not reflect the man I used to know—a man of integrity and honor."

Capri leaned back, folded her arms behind her head, and stretched her legs out in front of her. "Dip someone in a pot of spaghetti sauce, or, in this case, the political swamp, and they're likely going to get all red." When everyone gave her a confused look, she quietly added, "Okay, bad analogy. But, nice guy or not, he's cooked."

Lila took Reva's hands in her own. "We're your safe place. Tell us how this is impacting you—not Merritt or his career or reputation—you." She pointed to Reva's heart. "In here."

That's all it took. Reva's eyes flooded with tears.

"Oh, honey—what is it?" Charlie Grace asked, concern lacing her voice.

Their good friend glanced between all of them as if testing to see if she could say what was on her mind.

Lila gave her hands another squeeze. "We're here for you."

Reva nodded, then swallowed. "It's just—well, all the second-guessing. The what ifs. Frankly? I have such a good life.

I'm rich in many ways, but mostly in relationships with dear people I care about deeply and who care for me. I have meaningful work—work that makes a difference."

Capri nodded with enthusiasm. "Thunder Mountain couldn't get along without Reva Nygard."

Charlie Grace met Reva's gaze. "But?"

"But I thought I'd be married by now. I wanted children." A heaviness seemed to lift right off her shoulders as she admitted the fact to her girlfriends. Her expression took on a relieved look. She'd been carrying the weight of this hurt for some time.

Reva took a deep breath, her eyes shimmering. "And I know it's not too late, but sometimes, it feels like my chances are slipping away. There's not exactly a huge pool of candidates walking the wooden sidewalks of Thunder Mountain." She looked around at her friends, their faces a mix of empathy and love.

Lila leaned forward, her voice soft but firm. "Reva, your life, your dreams—they're not on a timetable. Love, family, children —they can happen at any time."

Capri poured herself another glass of wine. "So, Lila. Are you willing to subscribe to the notion you could fall in love again?"

Lila leaned back thoughtfully. "Well, I can't imagine it. But I hope so...someday."

Reva's mouth lifted in a slight smile. "None of us are exactly huge winners in the romance category."

"Hey," Charlie Grace interrupted. "I'm doing okay."

Capri resealed the wine bottle, a playful glint in her eye. "Oh yes, your little hook-up with McDreamy? Epic!"

Charlie Grace sighed deeply. "His name is Nick Thatcher," she reiterated, a note of exasperation in her voice. "And what I have with Nick, it's more than just a fling."

With a knowing chuckle, Capri winked at her friend. "Glad to hear it. I was just making sure."

Reva leaned back and wiped at her cheek. "Like Charlie Grace, I want more. I'm looking for someone to spend my life with. Someday, I long to gaze into an infant's eyes and promise I will love that baby forever." She groaned. "I'm getting to an age where pregnancy is no longer promised."

Lila rubbed the back of her neck. "Warning—those babies grow up into teenagers. I'm just saying."

That brought a laugh from Reva. "I know my dream is not a panacea. I don't care. I want it. I want it all." She glanced between them with a poignant look. "You can't control your heart."

Capri kicked her shoes off and tucked her feet up under her on the sofa. "Not everyone is meant for that route. Take me, for example."

Reva frowned. "You don't want to fall in love and have a family?"

Capri shrugged. "I'm working on falling in love with the life I have."

Charlie Grace reached out, placing a hand over Reva's. "You're not alone in this. We've all had our 'what-ifs' and 'if-onlys.' We can all claim our lives took turns we didn't expect—or wanted. But look at us—stronger and closer than ever. I hope you get it all, Reva—every bit of that dream. Regardless, we're here for you. No matter what is ahead."

Reva looked at each of her friends, her face filled with gratitude. "I don't know what I'd do without all of you. Thank you for reminding me that it's okay to feel this way and that I'm not alone." She grinned. "Even if you guys get a little pushy sometimes."

Lila took a sip of her wine. It was true.

The people that are still with you at the end of the day—those are the ones worth keeping. Sure, sometimes close can be too close. But sometimes, that invasion of personal space can be exactly what you need.

"Men can be fickle pickles," came her answer and a second look of solace.

Verna's charm lay in her sincere dedication and unwavering loyalty to her job and to Reva. Despite her aversion to modern technology, she somehow managed to keep the mayor's office and Reva's law practice both running like clockwork. Still, at times the gray-haired woman talked in cryptic messages and had trouble getting to the point.

Reva gathered her patience. "I'm sorry, Verna. You're going to have to explain."

Verna let the tall stack of papers drop to Reva's wooden desk with a thud. She placed a hand on Reva's arm. "Merritt Hardwick was never worthy of you. The entire town realized that when he took off for that fancy political career. According to the morning news, you were lucky to escape his clutches." She shook her head and slid into Reva's guest chair. "Oh, yes—he's extremely handsome. And charming. What politician isn't? If he did those awful things—and it sounds like he sure did—well, as Pastor Pete preaches, sin has a way of finding you out." She jabbed her finger in Reva's direction. "He deserves any punishment coming his way."

Verna let her finger weapon drop to her side. "Believe me, everyone at the Rustic Pine agrees!"

Reva's brows drew into a deep frown. "The Rustic Pine?"

"Oh, yes," her assistant told her. "The Knit Wits even took their coffee to go so they could scurry off to Moose Chapel."

Reva made her way behind her desk. She picked up the stack of papers and began fingering through them, trying to hide her discomfiture. "I'm not following."

"They are forming a prayer circle for you," Verna explained.

That got her attention. She groaned out loud. "The ladies are praying for me? Why?"

Verna's only response was to roll her eyes and sigh. She looked right at her and said, "That man is so low he couldn't

6

The older Reva got, the more she realized there was never enough time to accomplish everything she needed to get done. Juggling both her role as mayor of Thunder Mountain and her law practice meant she wore a lot of hats.

Her fairness and ability to listen to all sides of an issue had served her well in both roles.

Service was her hallmark, and she loved serving the residents of Thunder Mountain.

Yet, there were downsides to being so deeply invested in her community. Admittedly, she struggled to maintain boundaries with well-meaning people who were like GPS for gossip—always re-routing into someone else's lane.

Reva had no more than hung up her jacket in her office and hadn't even had a chance to sit down when one of them entered and marched directly to her desk.

"Oh, honey—I heard. And I'm so sorry."

Her dedicated assistant, Verna Billingsley, stood with a stack of papers in her hands, her face filled with sympathy.

"What are you talking about, Verna?"

jump off a dime. But ain't that the way it often is with love? We always fall for the bad boys." She shook her head, commiserating. "The rotten apples are not easy to get over."

Reva's heart gave three sharp thuds against her chest, but she managed to remain calm as she moved into her office chair. "I'm over Merritt Hardwick. Have been for a long time."

Verna raised her eyebrows. "Oh? Nicola Cavendish reports that early yesterday morning a man who looked very similar to Merritt was seen driving down Main Street in a rental car. The car was coming from the direction of your house."

Reva's breath caught.

"Oh, honey. Don't worry. Oma and the other Knit Wits told her to hush."

Reva struggled to swallow. "Well, to make the record straight—he only came to town saying he wanted me to know before the news broke. That's all. I was as surprised as anyone that he felt the need to tell me any of this. We went our separate ways years ago. Regardless of recent events, Merritt Hardwick is no longer a part of my life." She paused and looked her assistant directly in the eye leaving no room for argument. "I guarantee nothing has changed." Not that it was anyone's business, but it was better to clarify the situation and nip the rumor mill in the bud.

"Well, that's a relief to hear."

This conversation was going nowhere but down a path Reva did not want to tread. "Look, as much as my former love life is the talk of the town, I have a divorce hearing in less than two hours. I need to prepare."

Verna slapped her forehead. "Did I forget to tell you that the hearing is canceled? Apparently, Richard French spent last night with his soon-to-be ex-wife." She leaned forward, a hint of irony in her voice. "It seems Richard managed to fare slightly better than Merritt. He and Donna called this morning to report they're going to try and make a go of things."

"Well, that's good news," Reva muttered as she turned her computer on. Even better news was she just gained a couple of hours and could do some catch-up.

She opened her email folder and scanned the contents for any matters that needed immediate attention, then noticed her assistant was still sitting there looking across the desk at her. "Anything else, Verna?"

"Oh, no—that's it." She stood and remained in place for several seconds more before she added, "I'll be right out at my desk if you need me."

Reva pushed a stoic smile onto her face. "Okay, that's great. Thanks, Verna."

One more look of pity snuck across the woman's face before she turned and left the office, closing the door behind her.

Reva leaned back in her chair and pinched the bridge of her nose with her fingers. So, Merritt had been spotted leaving her place.

Great! Just great.

For the next several hours, Reva forced her attention on work. There was a stack of bids for the community center that needed her review and she had to draft a response to their county assessor, Merck Taylor. Every year, he got a little heavy-handed in his valuations and needed to be encouraged to pull back a bit, lest her constituents come off the rails after receiving their annual tax bills.

It was after two o'clock in the afternoon when her stomach growled, alerting her she'd worked right through lunch. Knowing her tummy would only grow more demanding if she tried to ignore the hunger signals, she turned off her laptop, scooped up her purse, and headed out. "Verna, I'm going to go grab a bite."

Verna shut down her iPad and scooped a few leftover sandwich crumbs from her desk into her palm, but not before Reva caught a bit of the gray-haired woman's favorite soap opera. She bragged she'd never missed an episode of *Guiding Light* and was now watching reruns of the defunct program on YouTube.

She looked up from the remains of her sandwich. "I just love that Lillian Raines, don't you?" she told Reva, who chose to look the other way as her boss. Verna might stretch her lunch hour a bit but was careful to always put in her eight hours of service daily.

A short walk later Reva entered the Rustic Pine and greeted the owners on her way to a bar stool. "Hey, Pete. Annie." Thankfully the bar was nearly empty this time of the day.

"Afternoon, Reva." Annie wiped her hands on a bar towel. "We're out of the special, but Pete can whip you up anything off the menu. That meatloaf always sells out fast."

Reva didn't need to scan the menu. Like most people in Thunder Mountain, she had the selections memorized. "How about a club sandwich?"

"Want fries with that?" Annie asked.

Normally, Reva would skip the calories. But after the morning she'd had, the indulgence was welcome. "Sure." She pointed to the glass case displaying the desserts. "And maybe a slice of that coconut pie."

The television mounted on the far wall flashed a familiar face, catching Reva's immediate attention. "Pete, would you mind turning that up?"

"Sure thing." He grabbed the remote from behind the counter and pointed it at the TV. The screen turned to a spokesman noted to be with the Justice Department standing behind a podium. "While we understand the public's interest in this matter, it is important to remember that the investigation is ongoing, and all individuals are presumed innocent until proven guilty in a court of law. We are committed to ensuring that justice is served fairly and impartially. Further details will be provided as they become available."

Despite having steeled herself for all of this, the media

announcement made things real. No longer were her thoughts circling Merritt's private confession to her. Now, he'd been officially charged, and the legal process had begun in earnest.

She listened for several more minutes, taking in the details as Merritt's image filled the television screen again. There were photographs of his campaign run, clips from the night he delivered his victory speech, and pictures of him and his family.

Reva finally looked away. "You can turn it off, Pete."

He gave her a sympathetic wink and complied. "You know, the good Lord has a way of bringing prodigals home," he reminded. His black lab, named Bartender, circled from behind the counter and barked his approval.

Reva nodded. Before she could respond, a voice from behind her rang out.

"You bet. Sounds like that boy woke up with his face buried in mud. Sadly, he won't be getting out of that pigpen anytime soon."

The entrance door opened, and Reva turned to see Nicola Cavendish walking in her direction, her purse perched in the crook of her elbow.

Annie called over to Pete who was at the grill. "Make that order to go, Pete." Reva gave her a grateful look.

"So," Nicola's nasal voice rang out. "It must be devastating to learn the love of your life is about to go to prison." Her knowing smile was as sharp as glass slivers. It would take some maneuvering not to get sliced.

Reva brought out her widest smile and glued it firmly in place. "Hello, Nicola."

While petite in stature, the woman's presence was large in Thunder Mountain. She carried herself with a self-assured air, convinced of her indispensable role in their community. She was the keeper of the town's pulse, the curator of its secrets. In her mind, her insights and revelations were as crucial to the town's identity as its landmarks.

"Did Merritt Hardwick come seeking legal advice? Or—" She paused. "Perhaps consolation?" Her suggestion was pregnant with not-so-hidden meaning.

"Merritt Hardwick came to town because he's too stupid for words."

They all turned to see Capri standing inside the door, her hands on her hips. "He may have wanted to run into his past to escape his dim future, but let me assure you, Reva is certainly not dwelling in bygone days. In fact, she's got a date this weekend."

Reva's eyes widened.

"As far as Merritt Hardwick being the love of Reva's life, I can tell you most assuredly that she has plowed that field and replanted." She turned and met Reva's shocked gaze. "Right, girlfriend?"

Reva swallowed and for some unexplained reason, she nodded.

"Oh, well, that's wonderful!" Insincerity dripped from Nicola's lips. "Reva has so much to offer."

Nothing irked Reva more than being spoken of in the third person, as if she wasn't standing right there hearing every word.

"Order up," Pete called out, a little louder than normal.

Annie scooped up the bag of food and walked it to Reva. "Here's your order, sweetie. I know you said you were in a hurry."

Thankful, Reva reached for the food. "Yeah, I've got an appointment." It wasn't a lie. She had an appointment to get out of Nicola's presence as quickly as possible.

Capri took the bag from her hands and opened it. "Hope you ordered enough to share." She said it as she headed for the door, leaving Reva scrambling to follow.

"Thanks, Pete. Thanks, Annie," she called over her shoulder.

Outside, she immediately scolded her good friend. "What

were you thinking telling Nicola I have a date? Do you not believe she'll camp out to see who it is?"

Capri grinned. "That's why the girls and I talked after leaving your place last night. We decided we needed to take action."

"Action?" The look on her friend's face suggested sinister intent.

Reva's expression shifted from surprise to disbelief as Capri unveiled their scheme. "We may have done something a bit... bold," she admitted, her voice tinged with a hint of guilt. "We set up an online dating profile for you."

Reva's shock quickly turned to irritation. Her friends meddling in her love life without her consent was more intrusive than endearing. "That was not a good idea," she insisted.

"No, listen. It's perfect. The alternative is to continue to weather the Knit Wit prayer circles and Nicola Cavendish's digs until something more interesting replaces their focus on you and Merritt."

Capri pulled up her phone. Her thumbs worked quickly to pull up the profile they had concocted, showcasing a carefully chosen photo of Reva and a bio that was more their words than hers.

Reva's discomfort grew as she looked over Capri's shoulder. She couldn't believe they would go this far without asking her. Despite Capri's enthusiasm, she immediately put up a wave of resistance when she was shown the message from a guy who seemed like a great match. She shook her head vehemently. "I am not going out on a date with a stranger."

A sense of disapproval crept over her, manifesting in a tight frown. The idea of going along with this charade felt dishonest, and it wasn't her style.

"Oh, c'mon. What's the worst that could happen? You might even have fun. I mean, when was the last time you went out on a date, Reva? No wonder speculation about you and Merritt is rampant."

Reva took a deep breath. The girls had crossed a line. Still, Capri had a point. Word would spread quickly and might quash the notion that she was still in any way interested in Merritt Hardwick.

Yes, her heart was broken. On multiple levels after hearing what her former fiancé had done. Honesty was her hallmark, and this plan seemed deceitful.

"You don't have much choice, do you?" Capri scrolled to the guy's photo. "And he's cute." She shoved the phone into Reva's hand so she could get a better look.

The guy wasn't hard to look at. She'd give Capri that much.

She thumbed through his information. Bert Reilly. Recently moved to Jackson Hole and worked remotely as an insurance actuary. More, he was the director of actuarial services. He had to be fairly educated to have a position at that level. He enjoyed the outdoors. Had a dog. Divorced.

"It's one date," Capri urged. "Snap a few pics of the two of you together, post on social media and voilà. Problem solved."

Problem solved.

She did like the sound of that.

7

Reva checked her reflection in the rearview mirror one last time before stepping from her Escalade onto the pavement. She shook her head, wondering again why she'd agreed to an online date, then drew a deep breath and headed for the entrance to the Gun Barrel Steak and Game House.

The drive to Jackson Hole had taken about forty-five minutes—time enough to conjure all the reasons why this ill-conceived date was a bad idea. First, Reva did not date—casually or otherwise. She didn't see the point. No one had captured her attention in that way since Merritt. Perhaps she was as picky as her girlfriends suggested, but need she point out that Thunder Mountain did not have a smorgasbord of dating options?

In their brief text exchange, she'd learned Bert Reilly had recently relocated from Los Angeles. Like so many people moving to their area lately, she suspected he wanted to escape the big city to enjoy a serene life in the mountains. If that were the case, she certainly couldn't blame him.

The Teton Mountains, with their dramatic peaks and pristine landscapes, called to the heart like a siren's song. Anyone lucky enough to call this area home was embraced by an ever-changing tapestry of natural beauty and adventure.

Her heels clicked against the concrete as she made her way up the steps to the door. Inside, the interior was themed to reflect the spirit of the Old West and the natural surroundings of Wyoming. Taxidermy animal mounts and antique firearms adorned the walls. The main dining space was spacious with a rustic yet elegant atmosphere. Weathered wooden beams, heavy leather upholstered chairs, and a massive stone fireplace gave the space the feel of a hunting lodge. But the centerpiece of the entire look was a life-sized mounted buffalo she knew from earlier visits the waiters introduced as Clyde.

Reva scanned the tables, feeling her nerves whittle at her normal confidence. Finally, against the wall sat a man who looked just like his online photo. He noticed her at the same time and waved.

She headed in that direction.

Upon her approach, he stood, a smile spreading across his face, radiating a warmth that matched the soft glow of the lights overhead. Her nervous state dissipated, replaced by a warm flutter of excitement and anticipation. Maybe this wasn't such a bad idea after all.

"Reva, it's so great to finally meet you," he said, his voice tinged with genuine enthusiasm. He offered a friendly handshake that lingered just a moment longer than expected, his eyes sparking with a mix of admiration and kindness. "You look wonderful," he added, his compliment sincere and effortless, as he gestured towards the table, inviting her to sit. The ease of his greeting, so natural and unpretentious, put Reva further at ease, igniting a hopeful spark for the evening ahead.

Suddenly, she was glad she'd taken the time to choose an outfit in a copper color that set off her eyes.

A waiter showed up at their table asking to take their drink orders.

"I'll have a glass of sparkling water with an orange twist," Reva told him.

Bert looked up at the waiter. "An old-fashioned for me—a double. Makers Mark. No ice with a dab of grated fresh ginger, a sprig of thyme, and served in a pre-chilled glass."

"Uh, I'll check and make sure we have fresh ginger," the waiter reported with an apologetic tone. "If we don't, is there a substitution I can make?"

Bert's eyes narrowed with disapproval. "You don't have fresh ginger?" He diverted his attention across the table to Reva. "What kind of nice restaurant doesn't have fresh ginger?"

Despite his rude comment, the waiter's expression didn't alter. "I'll check and see what we have available, sir."

"Thank you," Reva said.

He nodded, then moved from the table, leaving the two of them alone.

Bert knit his fingers and placed his palms on the table. "So, tell me all about yourself."

Reva took a breath, trying to recall what the girls had provided in her online profile. "Well, I grew up near here—in Thunder Mountain. I left after high school to attend Tulane, got my law degree, and hurried back home as fast as I could."

"Your profile says you are the mayor of Thunder Mountain?"

"Yes," she admitted, reluctant to be too open with her information. Stranger danger was a real thing. That's why she'd insisted on meeting in a public place.

"I looked you up," he explained.

Reva wished she'd thought to do the same. Maybe she wasn't cut out for this computer dating thing.

"I'm sorry, did I make you uncomfortable?" he asked, seeming to notice her discomfiture.

"I—well, this is my first online dating experience. I've never really gone out with a—"

"Stranger?" he offered.

She nodded and let a tiny smile drift onto her face. "Yes. Like I said, I'm new to this."

He waved off her concern. "I'm an old pro."

"Oh?" She tucked the information away. "Tell me about you. I mean, I read your profile information, but I'd like to know more."

"I'm in insurance." Before he could finish, his phone buzzed. He picked it up. "Hi, Mama. Yes, I'm here." He paused. "Yes, she's lovely. Just like her picture." He paused again, listening. "No, I won't eat any beef that is not grass-fed. No, I haven't had a chance to look over the menu, but I'm sure they have kale. If they do, I'll order a salad. Would you like me to bring some home to you?"

Bert never looked up as their drinks were delivered to the table, including the fresh ginger he wanted. He described the restaurant to his mother...in detail. "I'll bring you here sometime, Mama. You'll like it, I think."

Reva took a sip of her sparkling water and listened, trying not to scowl as she took in the conversation. Was he actually having an extended telephone visit with his mother while having dinner with her?

Minutes later, he finally hung up. "Sorry," he said as he placed his phone face up next to his napkin. "That was my mama."

"So, your mother lives in L.A.?" she asked.

"Oh, no. Mama moved to Jackson Hole with me."

Reva slowly nodded. "I see. Uh...any other family? I mean, is it just you and your mother?"

Over the course of the next few minutes, she learned Bert was an only child. He'd lost his father as a child to an accident. His mother's name was Leotha and she loved to cook, but only health-conscious items. Preservatives were of the devil. She also suffered from gout."

"Sounds like the two of you are...close?"

Bert beamed. "That would be affirmative. She's the most wonderful woman I've ever known. I'm a lucky boy."

Reva tried hard not to roll her eyes. The main course had not yet arrived, and this date was already shaping up to be unviable. Especially when Bert launched into detailing all the many gifts his mother had given him over the years, presents that included his most prized possession.

Reva listened, half-amused and half-bewildered, as Bert excitedly rambled about the metal detector his mother had gifted him last Christmas. He delved into the mundane specifics with an enthusiasm that she found perplexing, describing the length of its telescopic shaft, the diameter of the search coil, and the various beeping tones it emitted depending on the type of metal detected.

His eyes sparkled as he recounted the settings for differentiating between ferrous and non-ferrous metals, a detail that Reva noted with a nod, though she hardly understood why it mattered.

Then, Bert's monologue took a bizarre turn as he began to list the peculiar treasures he had unearthed—a collection of vintage bottle caps from the 1970s, a surprisingly well-preserved rubber duck with a metal collar, and, most baffling of all, a rusted keychain with a half dozen keys, each leading to an unknown lock.

Reva couldn't help but smile at the sheer oddity of his finds, wondering if the metal detector was a tool for unearthing treasures or a gateway into Bert's uniquely quirky world.

A world she couldn't wait to exit.

When the waiter appeared to take their orders, Reva ordered a bowl of soup—butternut squash topped with coconut and nutmeg foam. She could eat that fast and end this, maybe beg off with a headache if need be. Sitting on the sofa in her slippers with a good book sounded good right now.

Unfortunately, Bert was not in a hurry.

He slowly scanned the menu, asking dozens of questions. "How are your steaks cooked? On a grill or over an open flame?" He looked at Reva. "Grills are never cleaned properly. Mama says the metal leaches and attaches to the proteins in the meat. She read that in *Your Wellness Today* magazine."

He returned to grilling the waiter (no pun intended, she thought) before finally settling on bison ravioli—a dish described as served with white wine garlic sauce with cherry tomatoes and goat cheese. "But hold the cherry tomatoes," Bert said as he handed his menu off to the waiter. "And the goat cheese. I'd like a side of whipped sweet potato puree, but could you simply cut that into little square chunks and give me butter on the side? Unsalted butter if you have it. Bring a little extra."

The waiter nodded. Before he could finish lifting the menu from Bert's hand, her date suddenly changed his mind and held on to the printed board. Confused, the waiter raised his chin. "Is there something else you'd like, sir?"

"Dessert. Bring three servings of that bourbon pudding right there." He pointed to an item on the menu. "Make one of them to-go." He looked to Reva. "Mama loves bread pudding."

She held up an open hand. "None for me."

"Oh, c'mon. Those calories aren't going to put any more meat on your bones. Live a little."

Her jaw stiffened. "I don't do bourbon."

"Well, this isn't a drink. It's pudding."

"I don't drink," she clarified, her tone one that invited no more argument.

"What? You're an alcoholic?" He turned to the waiter and lifted his empty cocktail glass. "Speaking of, I'll have another, please."

When he turned back, Reva couldn't help but scowl. This man was proving to be rude, boring, *and* obnoxious.

He examined her expression. "Oh, hey—I'm sorry. So you're an alcoholic." He waved off the situation. "No problem. My mama's brother was a drunk. Cool guy. He died of liver cirrhosis."

Bert turned to the waiter. "Just box hers up, and I'll take it home with me."

Reva knotted her hands underneath the table. This date couldn't end fast enough. She fully intended to throttle those well-meaning friends of hers if they ever meddled in her romantic life again.

She suffered through the remainder of the meal, happy when the waiter finally brought the bill to the table.

Bert opened the black leather check holder, took a quick look inside, and handed it back to the waiter. "Could you split the check, please?"

"Yes, sir," the waiter replied, daring to sneak a sympathetic glance at Reva.

Reva felt her facial muscles tighten. She quickly retrieved her wallet and held out her credit card. "No, that's all right. I've got it covered," she offered. No way did she want to extend the time with this man, not even long enough for the bill to be recalculated.

Bert glanced at his Rolex. "I hope you don't mind ending our time together a little early. I promised Mama we'd watch *Northern Exposure* on Netflix. She's waiting for me."

"No, no...that's fine," she assured him.

He got out his phone and opened an app. "So, Reva. When do you want to do this again?"

8

"Ew...gross. Mom!"

"What?" Lila asked, slowly turning from her open laptop, distracted. She was studying last week's lesson and trying to catch up. Who knew you could administer physical therapy to giraffes to reduce knee socket pain? Of course, it wasn't like she'd be treating any exotics in Wyoming.

"Mom!" Camille complained loudly. She held up a tray of lidded glass vials filled with yellow liquid. "Tell me this isn't what I think."

Lila closed her laptop. "Those are urine samples. Shut the fridge door. The specimens need to be kept at a low temperature for the testing to be accurate."

Camille groaned. "Doesn't Doc Tillman have a refrigerator down at Paws in the Pines? I mean, really. This is disgusting."

Lila stood and lifted the tray from her daughter's hand then secured it back in place before shutting the door. "I didn't want to go back to the clinic this evening after the collection at the Bayer's place. Their litter of puppies haven't been eating and I wanted to rule out a few things before taking further measures."

"The little malamutes?"

Lila nodded. "Yes, and they are so cute. You should see them. Hopefully, I don't have to quarantine the tiny things. Their symptoms don't line up exactly with leptospirosis, but I don't want to take any chances. With all the wildlife around, a lot of water sources can be contaminated."

Her daughter wrinkled her nose and turned to the sink where she squirted some soap and scrubbed her hands with extra vigor. "So, you think it's a good idea to put that stuff next to the food we eat?" She shook her head. "Never mind—I'll just head into the Rustic Pine for dinner. Do you have a twenty?"

Lila kissed the top of her daughter's blonde head. "Every extra dollar I have this month is going to your prom dress. The fabric arrived, and Aunt Mo said she already started on your dress. She wants to do a sizing before she finishes up."

Charlie Grace's aunt was a multi-talented woman and was known for her seamstress ability. She'd made more prom and wedding dresses over the years than anyone could count.

Lila brightened. "The gown is ready to try on?" She clapped her wet hands together. "I can't wait to see it."

Her daughter had chosen a pattern fashioned after a designer garment she'd spotted online—a strappy floor-length dress in hot pink satin reminiscent of a gown you might see on a beauty pageant contestant...and far too sexy for a soon-to-be seventeen-year-old, in her mother's opinion.

Lila had learned to pick her battles. This wasn't one of them.

The argument regarding homemade versus store-bought had already exhausted her patience. Raising a teenage daughter alone wasn't cheap, and no way was she shelling out the big bucks for some retailer version when Aunt Mo could easily duplicate the style for so much less.

Lila's phone buzzed, signaling an incoming call. She held up a finger. "Sorry, honey. Let me get this."

"Hey, Charlie Grace. What's up? The calf still doing okay?"

"The calf is fine. But Reva's not. Our little plan didn't work out so well."

"What do you mean?"

Charlie Grace sighed. "The guy was a dud. An entitled doofer who still lives with his mother."

Lila frowned. "Oh, no."

"Yeah, all our high hopes dashed. The best we can expect is that our scheme at least tamped the rumor mill. Reva neglected to get any photos to post on social media. Her saving grace is that Brewster Findley was taking his wife out for an anniversary dinner and spotted them in the parking lot as he was pulling in. Word has already spread."

"Well, that's what we hoped for." Lila covered the phone speaker and whispered to her daughter, "Reva's date was a bust."

Camille rolled her eyes. "Serves you guys right for trying to hook her up in the first place. I told you the plan was lame." She reached behind her head and tucked her long hair into a messy bun at the nape of her neck.

Ignoring the jab, Lila returned her attention to the phone conversation. "So, do we take it down?"

"What down?" Charlie Grace asked.

"The dating profile."

There was a brief pause. "No, let's leave it up."

"She'll have our hide if we do."

Charlie Grace laughed. "Won't be the first time."

They were about to hang up when Lila said, "Wait...I forgot. You're hosting girlfriend night tomorrow, right?"

"Yeah," came Charlie Grace's answer. "Why?"

"Well, do you think Mo could join us? I mean, just this once. I'm juggling a lot right now, timewise, and she has the prom dress ready for Camille to try on. I can kill two birds with one stone."

"How ironic for a vet to be killing off birds! But sure, I'll check with Aunt Mo and the others. It's been a while since we all fawned over prom dresses."

On Friday night, they all gathered at Charlie Grace's place out at the Teton Trails Guest Ranch. This late in the spring, occupancy remained low until children were out of school and family vacation season started. This left the main lodge at their disposal.

Over at the family house, Charlie Grace's father, Clancy, had sweetly taken on the role of entertaining his granddaughter. He planned a fun evening of games, ensuring Charlie Grace he'd have Jewel tucked in bed at the proper time while Aunt Mo slipped away to join the group for the eagerly anticipated dress fitting.

With Camille by her side, Lila checked her watch and headed across the grass lawn, past the guest cabins, and in the direction of the lodge built of raw logs with a sprawling wraparound porch sporting rocking chairs and tables.

They climbed the stairs, crossed the porch, and opened the door.

"Hey, there you are," Charlie Grace called out, her voice tinged with excitement. She stood by the large stone fireplace, her figure slightly bent as she skillfully fed fresh logs to the crackling fire. Although summer was fast approaching, the mountain air still carried an occasional hint of winter chill.

"Champagne's waiting," Capri announced, pointing to the table lined with five pretty glass flutes and a tray of finger foods. A bottle was wedged in ice in a feeding bucket next to a couple of sodas.

Lila grinned and pointed. "Nice touch."

Capri laughed. "Beggars can't be choosers." She lifted the bottle and wrapped the top in a tea towel as she prepared to uncork it.

"Where's Mo?" Camille asked.

Charlie Grace dusted off her hands. "She'll be here anytime."

As if on cue, the door opened, and Mo appeared with a hot pink garment draped over her arm. Everyone greeted her as she laid the gown over the back of the leather sofa. "It's coming together nicely," she reported, then to Camille, "You ready to try it on?"

Camille enthusiastically nodded. "You bet."

"Okay, then. Follow me." Mo picked up the dress and headed up the stairs to where the vacant bedrooms were located.

Capri poured champagne and passed out the glasses. "Sure brings back memories, doesn't it?"

Reva took a soda. "Yeah, how can one of us have a daughter old enough to attend prom?"

Lila shook her head. "Tell me about it. My breath sometimes catches when I see Camille coming down the hall. To me, she's still that little toddler who used to say, 'In a knot, here I come.'"

Laughter rang out.

"I remember," Charlie Grace said. "That girl had the funniest sayings."

Reva popped the top of her soda can and drained the contents into a glass filled with ice. "Remember when she started the Lord's prayer with 'Our Father, who aren't in heaven?'"

The room resonated with more laughter as the girls settled comfortably onto the sofas. Capri drew her legs beneath her, a playful spark in her eyes. "Do you guys recall that year when I stubbornly chose a short prom dress just to stand out?"

Reva's eyes twinkled with amusement. "Oh, you mean that one with the rather...striking bow on the hip?"

"That was the year you went to the prom with the kid who

was so short, his nose seemed to settle right between your breasts when you danced," Charlie Grace reminded Lila.

Lila groaned. "Ugh, don't remind me." She took a sip of her champagne. "I wonder what ever happened to him. I don't even remember his name."

Charlie Grace lifted from her spot on the sofa and moved to the kitchen counter. She carried the tray of food to the coffee table and set it down, along with a stack of paper napkins. "Wasn't it Milton something?"

"Milton Barrett!" Capri cried out. "He moved in the spring of the following year with his folks."

"To Alaska," Reva added.

Capri nodded. "Yeah, that's right," she said, pausing as a reflective expression crossed her face. "He was odd."

Reva reached for a cheese-topped cracker. "Speaking of odd..."

Charlie Grace offered a sympathetic glance. "I heard your date didn't go exactly as planned," she said gently.

Reva sighed. A wry smile formed. "That's putting it mildly. Listen to this—for our second date, he proposed we go treasure hunting with his metal detector."

"He sounds like a keeper," Capri teased with a playful roll of her eyes. She turned to Charlie Grace. "That was the same year you snuck out with Gibbs Nichols. We all had to lie for you when your dad showed up early at the gymnasium to drive the two of you home."

Reva scowled. "Drive you home? Why didn't Gibbs take you home?"

Charlie Grace chuckled. "He'd temporarily lost his driver's license for drag racing out at the garbage dump, remember?" She refilled her champagne glass, nearly letting the bubbly spill over the top of her flute. "Too bad Gibbs wasn't the one who moved to Alaska. Would have saved me a lot of headaches. The only good thing to come out of that marriage was my sweet

Jewel. She made it all worth it." She swiftly brought the glass to her lips, taking a quick sip to prevent the champagne from spilling over and causing a mess.

"By the way," she added. "I'm giving a baby shower for Lizzy. I want you all to come."

Reva's eyebrows lifted. "You're throwing a shower for your ex-husband's wife? After you caught them in the hay...literally?"

Charlie Grace's shrug was nonchalant. "Life moves on, and so have I," she said with a lightness that belied the depth of her journey. "Besides, holding onto grudges is like carrying old, heavy luggage—it just slows you down. Lizzy and I have found a way to coexist, for Jewel's sake. And well, every baby deserves a celebration, right?"

The others exchanged glances, a mix of surprise and admiration in their eyes.

Capri leaned forward, her tone laced with respect. "That's incredibly big of you, Charlie Grace. I mean, with the history you have with Gibbs and all that drama, it's amazing how you're able to just let it go and extend such a gesture." She looked at the others. "Girls think they can fix him....but it'd take an entire construction crew to overhaul that bag of nothing."

Charlie Grace raised her glass slightly, the light from the fire catching the champagne's effervescence. "True, but here's to new beginnings and burying old hatchets. Life's too short for anything less."

The soft crackling of the fire filled the room as Charlie Grace's words lingered, prompting a contemplative silence.

After a few seconds, Capri lifted her flute in the air. "Yes, here's to old proms and bright futures."

With a collective sigh, they clinked their glasses in a quiet salute to the heart's resilience and the promise of bright days ahead.

9

Reva glanced at her Escalade's dashboard clock, noting she was a full fifteen minutes early for her meeting. Her girlfriends called her penchant for punctuality quirky. Perhaps, but her habit of arriving early was practical and afforded her precious time she used to tick tasks off her ever-present list.

Among today's priorities was reaching out to Carlene Baker, a valued member of her community facing health concerns. Delving into her bag, Reva retrieved her phone to send Carlene a message, kindly offering a ride for Carlene's doctor's appointment the next day.

Carlene's response was immediate, tinged with polite refusal. "Oh, that's not necessary. You're far too busy. I can drive."

Reva knew better. Carlene, with her white hair and petite frame, struggled to peer over the steering wheel due to severe osteoporosis, which had further diminished her already small stature.

With a smile, Riva quickly tapped out a firm reply. "Nonsense, I'll be there at eleven."

Turning off her phone, Reva's mind shifted to her schedule, mentally calculating the time needed to return from her morning hearing to fulfill her promise to Carlene.

A tap on her window drew her attention. She pressed the button and waited for the glass to lower. "Hey, Van. What's up?"

"The doors are locked. You have a key, right?"

"Yeah." She frowned, puzzled. "It's usually open."

Just as she said it, a blue pickup pulled into the gravel parking lot. George Argyle scrambled out and held up a set of keys. "Sorry, everyone. Got held up with some bears crossing the highway. Damn tourists stopped, got out of their cars with cameras and phones, and stood right in the middle of the road, blocking it."

He murmured a quiet curse, his footsteps leading him toward the entrance of Moose Chapel. Reva trailed behind Van, her curiosity piqued by his grouchy nature. "How's the week been treating you, Van?"

Adjusting his John Deere cap, Van shared his plight. "My lawnmower's given up on me. Had to order parts, and they won't arrive till next week. The missus is keen on having the lawn trimmed, but it seems she'll have to be patient a bit longer." A shadow of frustration flickered across his face as he spoke.

Reva smiled. Van's relationship with his wife was legendary. He would move the Tetons into the sea to make her happy.

She plucked her phone back out of her purse. "Tell you what, I'll make a quick call," she said decisively. Not pausing for his response, she swiftly dialed a number and pressed the phone to her ear, anticipating the voice that would soon greet her from the other end.

"Hey, Reva. What's up?"

"Hey, Merck. Is your kid still mowing lawns to raise money for his football camp?"

"Yeah, why?"

"Tell him to show up at Van Bennett's tomorrow with his lawnmower and trimmer. I'll pay him extra if he does a good job."

"You bet," Merck said. "I'll send him over. Thanks, Reva."

Reva clicked off the call and turned to Van, smiling. "You tell that sweet wife she doesn't have to wait."

Van shook his head. "You didn't have to do that, Reva. And to make things clear, I can pay for my own lawn to be mowed."

"Yes, I know. This is my gift." She drew him into a shoulder hug as they made their way inside and down the stairs to the basement. "If my offer still bothers you, simply pay the favor forward to someone else."

The room was lined with folding chairs. Against the back wall stood a long table covered with a disposable tablecloth topped with a large box filled with donuts and maple bars on one end. On the other end, paper coffee cups and a basket filled with packets of sugar and creamer were neatly arranged next to a stainless-steel coffee urn.

Dick Jacobs, Capri's stepfather, scanned the donut box and lifted a chocolate-covered one onto a napkin. He turned. "Can I get you a maple bar, Reva?"

She smiled back at him. "No thanks, Dick." She pointed to her hips. "Watching my figure."

That brought a smile to his face. "Me, too." He followed up the statement with a bite of donut.

Dick had lost a tremendous amount of weight during his recent cancer treatments when he was unable to eat. She was glad to see his appetite had returned.

Reva made her way past a row of empty chairs and sat next to Dorothy Montgomery, who proudly held her one-year coin in her hands.

"Well, look at that," Reva remarked, pointing to it.

Dot beamed. "You work the program, and the program works

for you." The phrase underscored the idea that active participation and commitment to the Alcoholics Anonymous program's principles and steps were crucial for achieving and maintaining sobriety.

Reva reached and squeezed her hand. "Yes, every one of us in here knows that to be true."

Minutes later, the meeting began. Reva grabbed her well-worn and dog-eared copy of the Big Book from her purse and headed for the podium. "Hey, everyone...let's take our seats."

The small assembly at the back quietly settled into their chairs.

Reva opened her book and began to read aloud the evening's presentation, focusing on the theme of surrendering control and acknowledging that not everything is within one's power to manage.

As her voice filled the room, the words resonated inside her. These principles felt particularly poignant tonight as she had been wrestling with her feelings over Merritt's surprise revelations earlier this week.

While she was no longer in love with Merritt, Reva's instinct was to steer herself clear of the emotional storm of his choices. But her desire to manage the outcome of Merritt's decisions was an exercise in futility. The only power truly hers was in how she chose to respond—an insight she illuminated during open sharing time.

As the last of the personal stories and reflections tapered off, the room grew quiet. Reva's voice, steady and clear, broke the silence. "God, grant us the serenity to accept the things we cannot change, the courage to change the things we can, and the wisdom to know the difference."

A unified "Amen" filled the room.

The Serenity Prayer, a personal anchor for Reva, resonated deeply within her. How often had these words served as a balm for her soul, especially during the challenging early stages of her journey toward sobriety? And how often did they continue to provide comfort?

As the room slowly emptied, the sound of laughter and snippets of conversations lingered, a testament to the strength and support found within these walls.

The next morning, Reva set out for a hike around Jenny Lake, continuing to embrace the peace that the prayer instilled in her. The serene beauty of the surroundings, coupled with the early morning calm, provided a perfect backdrop for reflection.

As she meandered along the path lined with towering pine trees, Reva found the words of the Serenity Prayer reverberating in her consciousness, a soothing testament to her inner fortitude and personal evolution. Each stride brought with it a wave of gratitude for the path she had chosen, one paved with resilience and transformative growth—fortified over years of brave introspection and healing.

The recent upheaval brought by Merritt's visit and his startling revelations might have once shattered her. She, no doubt, would have sought refuge in the numbing embrace of vodka, drowning her escalating vulnerability in a sea of alcohol until consciousness slipped away.

But that was a chapter of her life she closed long ago. That Reva, who cowered from the reality of her limitations, who believed she could mend every fracture in her world, was no more.

Today, she stood as a woman who, while still instinctively nurturing others, prioritized her own well-being above all. She made a solemn vow to herself—she would never revert to the days of drowning her insecurities in drink, steadfast in her journey of sobriety and self-care.

Despite her resolve, the sight of Merritt's face plastered across every magazine at every newsstand still cut deep. Reva couldn't help but feel a pang of deep sorrow for his choices and the inevitable repercussions that he and his family would face. The constant media exposure was a harsh reminder of the complex tapestry of human character—a paradox of virtue and vice, all coexisting in the same soul.

Reva continued her walk along the serene shore, taking in the gentle lapping of the lake's waters against the pebbled shore and the soft rustle of quaking aspen leaves in the gentle breeze. The air was crisp and invigorating, carrying the fresh, earthy scent of pine and the subtle, sweet fragrance of balm weed and balsamroot that speckled the nearby meadows.

Each breath filled her lungs with a sense of renewal as she sat on a large lava rock, taking in the way the majestic Teton Range reflected in the lake's mirror-like surface. Sunlight dappled through the canopy of tall pines, adding to the tranquil ambiance.

This was her place—a haven for her soul.

Reva's interlude was interrupted by a sudden rustle of leaves and the soft thud of paws on earth. A golden retriever, its coat shimmering in the sunlight, bounded into view and ran towards her with unbridled enthusiasm.

"Max, heel!" called a voice, rich and slightly amused.

A man emerged from the dappled shade of the trees, his approach marked by the crunch of pine needles and leaves underfoot. He wasn't the kind of man who'd turn heads with his striking looks, but there was an undeniable allure in his unassuming presence. His eyes, clear and honest, met hers with an intensity that seemed to acknowledge her in a way words couldn't.

"Oh, I'm so sorry," he said, as the dog's leash tangled around Reva's legs and he pounced onto her lap, licking her face. "Max, get down!"

"It's okay." Reva laughed. "He's quite friendly, isn't he?"

"Too friendly sometimes," the man admitted, carefully

untangling the leash. His hands brushed against hers. "I hope he didn't startle you."

"Not at all, I love dogs. He's beautiful." Her hands stroked the dog's furry back as its tail wagged wildly.

"I'm guessing he's made a new friend," the man said, smiling softly.

"I'm Reva," she stood and introduced herself, extending a hand.

"Nice to meet you, Reva. I'm Kellen Warner." His voice was friendly yet firm and held a note of something unspoken, an undercurrent of connection she couldn't quite define.

Hating to be caught in an awkward stare, she diverted her gaze to his dog. "So, Max...do you live in these parts, or are you just visiting?" She surprised herself by holding her breath, waiting for the answer she hoped to hear as she looked back up at him.

He rubbed the side of his trimmed goatee. "We live just outside Jackson Hole, on a little place in Wilson."

"Wilson? That's where they are filming that new television show, *Bear Country*. My girlfriend is dating the production designer," she explained.

"Yeah, it's quite the deal."

The way he said it left her wondering how he felt about the situation.

A chipmunk, tiny and agile, suddenly darted across the path, its quick movements a blur of brown and gray. It scampered with lightning speed, tiny paws skittering over the hard-packed earth as it navigated the terrain with ease.

Max perked up at the sight. With a burst of canine enthusiasm, he lunged forward, his golden fur rippling in the sunlight as he gave chase. The chipmunk zigzagged with incredible agility, disappearing into the underbrush, leaving Max to pause and look around, his tail wagging in the excitement of the brief and spirited pursuit.

Reva and Kellen both laughed.

"Well, we should be heading on," Kellen said, tucking the leash under his arm and calling Max to his side.

"Yes, Kellen and Max, it was lovely meeting you both," Reva said as they prepared to part ways.

"Likewise," Kellen replied, a hint of reluctance in his tone. "Take care, Reva."

As Kellen and Max walked away, Reva stood for a moment, watching them go. The encounter had been brief, but it left an impression. There was something about Kellen, in the way his eyes held hers, in the timbre of his voice, that resonated with her.

With a thoughtful smile, she continued her walk, the memory of their meeting lingering.

10

Reva climbed from her car, taking in the early morning sunlight as it spilled over the Tetons in the distance, their jagged peaks piercing the sky like spires of a cathedral. She could live to be one hundred and never tire of the beauty of this area.

She pulled a hard hat from the back seat of her Escalade and secured it to her head. Clutching rolled-up architectural plans under her arm, she made her way to the building site where pine-covered acreage would soon transform into the heartbeat of Thunder Mountain, the new community center.

The air was crisp and filled with the smell of freshly cut pine trees tinged with the earthy scent of fresh dirt. In the distance, a bulldozer rumbled into action its blade pushing topsoil aside with effortless might, carving a path through the meadow.

Reva approached the group of architects and contractors gathered around a makeshift table littered with blueprints and site maps. "Good morning, everyone," she said, her voice steady and clear. "Today, we lay the groundwork for not just a building, but our town's future. Let's make sure we're all aligned on the vision and schedule."

Constructing a community center represented a bold endeavor for their modest town, serving as a powerful testament to their deep-seated commitment to fostering connections among its residents.

Alex, the lead architect from the firm in Cheyenne, unrolled the main blueprint across the table, anchoring the corners with stones. "This is the comprehensive layout of the community center, incorporating your early thoughts, Mayor." He pointed to the detailed sketches. "We've designed it to be not only functional but a symbol of the community of Thunder Mountain and what makes your town unique."

Reva leaned in, tracing the lines of the blueprint with her finger. "I see we have a large central hall, meeting rooms, and what's this area here?" She tapped a section of the plans. "That's the community garden space you suggested," Alex explained, his eyes lighting up with enthusiasm. "We'll place the garden benches here and here." He pointed. "With the fountain right here."

The scent of fresh coffee mingled with the morning air as a contractor holding a steaming mug piped in, "We started site excavation yesterday. It's crucial we stick to the timeline to ensure we meet our deadline of completion, especially if you hope to open on schedule." His tone was pragmatic, underscoring his dedication to the project.

Reva nodded, absorbing every detail. "And the materials, are we still on track for sourcing locally as much as possible?"

Alex nodded. "Yes, Mayor. We're coordinating with local suppliers for timber and stone. And we're open to hiring from the community."

She nodded, satisfied. "That's perfect. I'll coordinate through my office if you like."

Their discussion continued, covering everything from energy-efficient lighting to accessible design, punctuated by the soft rustling of the plans as Alex flipped through page after page while highlighting the concepts captured in their work.

As the meeting concluded, the group stood together, surveying the empty lot, now alive with the potential of what was to come.

"I'm thrilled with these plans," Reva said. The clinking of coffee cups filled the air as her gaze swept over the faces around her. "Let's build something that will stand as a cornerstone of our community for generations."

With a final nod of agreement, the team dispersed, leaving Reva standing on the site, the plans in her hand no longer just paper, but the blueprint of a dream about to be realized. The sound of departing vehicles and the whispering breeze through the pines followed her to her car.

Sitting in the driver's seat with the door open, Reva replaced mud-covered boots with heels and prepared to head to the courthouse. She had a brief hearing and then planned to pick up Carlene and drive her to her doctor's appointment, as promised.

Her hand reached for the ignition button when the distant wail of sirens sliced through the calm morning air, instantly knotting her stomach with concern. The siren's cry was not just a sound but a signal that someone in her community was in distress.

Her brows furrowed in worry as she instinctively reached for her phone to check for any emergency alerts or messages. Even as she sat there, momentarily stalled by the piercing sounds, her mind raced through potential scenarios, calculating her next steps and the resources that might be needed.

Was it a fire? An accident?

Her phone rang, and she immediately took the call from

the town deputy. "Fleet, what have we got?" she asked, her voice laced with concern.

"An accident north of town. I'm on my way."

"I'll meet you there," she said, silently lifting a prayer for the people involved.

Reva threw her SUV into gear and spun her vehicle around. As she raced towards the source of the sirens, the scene outside her car windows shifted to the familiar businesses lining Main Street where townspeople were gathered on the wooden sidewalks, their faces etched with shared concern and turning their attention to the commotion.

She pressed her foot down on the gas pedal. Soon, vibrant, green meadows marked the transition to the more rugged outskirts north of Thunder Mountain, the tranquility disrupted by flashing lights in the far distance.

The further she drove, the more pronounced the sense of emergency became, with the road narrowing and the dense canopy of pine trees giving way to an open stretch where the accident had unfolded. Ahead, the chaos of flashing lights, emergency vehicles, and the first responders moving with purposeful speed painted a stark contrast against the serene backdrop of the Teton Mountains, their presence a silent witness to the unfolding drama below.

As Reva's vehicle skidded to a halt at the edge of the crash scene, she jumped out wishing she had not changed into heels. Her heart pounded in her chest as she surveyed the scene before her, a maelstrom of activity—paramedics from the hospital in Jackson darting between twisted metal, firefighters cutting through the wreckage, and police officers cordoning off the area. The air was thick with the smell of gasoline, the sound of urgent shouts of the first responders, and the hiss of extinguishing flames.

"Mayor, it's bad." A grim-faced police officer approached

her, his voice heavy with sorrow. "We've got fatalities. The license plates...they're not from around here."

His words hung in the air as Reva's gaze swept the scene, her heart sinking with each detail—pieces of twisted metal and glass littering the pavement, skid marks on the highway, a lone shoe—until it landed on a sight that clenched her heart in a vise.

Fleet Southcott stood by the side of the road, holding a tiny toddler in his arms. The child, miraculously unscathed but bewildered, clung to the officer, a stark image of innocence amidst chaos.

Reva's throat tightened, tears stinging her eyes as she moved closer, her role as mayor momentarily eclipsed by her humanity. "Is...is the child all right?" she managed to ask, her voice barely a whisper, as the reality of the situation—a family torn apart, a life spared while others were lost—washed over her.

Fleet nodded, his own eyes glistening with unshed tears. "Yes, Reva. But it looks like this little tyke lost everyone."

The impact of his statement hit her as Reva stood amidst the echoes of lost lives, barely able to breathe in the wake of the unfolding tragedy. Such a random, senseless situation—a poignant reminder of the fragility of life and the indiscriminate nature of fate.

Suddenly the tiny toddler reached for her with chubby outstretched arms the color of her own—a silent plea for comfort.

Instinct kicked in and Reva lifted the little boy from Fleet's arms and held him tightly against her chest. "Shhh...everything is going to be okay," she murmured, making a promise that sounded hollow as the words escaped her lips.

At that moment, the heavy weight of the tragedy burrowed deep inside her bones along with an unwavering duty not just to reassure but to protect and advocate for this tiny survivor in a world that had just ripped everything from him.

Reva leaned her cheek against the soft black coils of the baby boy's hair, silently vowing to spare no effort to turn her promise into reality.

She leaned down and picked up the single shoe on the pavement, a woman's shoe.

"I give you my word," she whispered.

11

Reva's heart pounded in her chest as she climbed into the ambulance, her arms cradling the toddler. The paramedics, a woman named Lisa and a mature man named Mark, worked efficiently, checking the child's vitals and ensuring he was stable.

"Is he going to be okay?" Reva's voice was laced with concern as she watched them.

"He's stable for now," Lisa replied, offering a reassuring smile. "A miracle, really."

As the ambulance sped toward the hospital in Jackson, the gravity of the situation dawned on Reva. She needed to act, to do more than just physically protect the child. Pulling out her phone, she dialed the only number she could think of at that moment.

"Hello?"

"Sam, it's Reva. I need your help."

Sam, a close friend who lived in Jackson and a fellow lawyer, sounded surprised. "Reva, what's wrong?"

"I'm in an ambulance. It's not me. I'm fine. But there was an accident, and I found a toddler. He's alone, Sam. His parents were lost in the crash. I vowed to protect him, but I don't know what to do next."

Sure, she'd practiced plenty of family law, but nothing like this. She'd never encountered taking care of a tiny orphan and what steps were required to meet the obligations before her.

There was a pause on the other end of the line. "Okay, first things first. You need to ensure he's treated at the hospital. Then they will likely contact Child and Family Services since he's unaccompanied. You should express your willingness to be a temporary guardian if necessary. It'll involve a lot of legal processes, but I can guide you through it."

"Thank you, Sam. I—I just couldn't leave him."

"I know. Just focus on getting him care. I'll start looking into what needs to be done on my end. He'll have family somewhere."

"I don't even know his name," Reva murmured.

"I'll see what I can do to gather some information. I'm looking at the sketchy details available online now. There will be more added. I'll report back anything I find."

After the call, Reva turned her attention back to the toddler, whispering words of comfort as the paramedics continued their work.

Upon arrival at the hospital, nurses and doctors swarmed around taking the child from Reva's arms to provide necessary medical attention. Feeling suddenly empty-handed, Reva followed as closely as she could, explaining the situation to anyone who would listen.

A hospital social worker approached, a kind-looking woman in her fifties who introduced herself as Mrs. Greene. "Can you tell me what happened?"

Reva recounted the events, the horrific accident, and the discovery of the toddler, including her phone call with Sam. Mrs. Greene listened intently, nodding along.

"You've done the right things," the woman assured. "We'll

need to contact Child and Family Services, as protocol dictates. However, given your involvement and willingness to help, I'll make sure to note that in my report. It could help in determining temporary guardianship or foster care arrangements until we locate any family he might have."

Reva nodded. "Please, let me know what I can do. I just want him to be safe."

"We will," she promised.

Reva took a seat in the waiting room, filled with a mixture of worry and determination. She'd stumbled into this situation by chance, but now she was deeply invested. Whatever it took, she was ready to fight for the well-being of the child she'd vowed to protect.

With Sam's legal guidance and the support of the hospital's staff, she wasn't alone in this unexpected journey. She'd also spent years on the board of directors of The Hope Project, a statewide initiative for adoption. This afforded her a unique perspective on the process and a network of connections that would be invaluable as she navigated the hours ahead.

As the clock on the wall ticked close to an hour since she'd arrived, Reva's phone buzzed with incoming texts. The first was from Capri. "I just heard. What can I do to help?"

Reva's thumbs moved deftly over the tiny screen. *"I'm in waiting mode. Need nothing at this point but additional information."* She typed out a request for Capri to pick up Carlene and get her to her appointment.

Capri quickly agreed. *"No worries. Will get it handled."*

Next, she called the court about her hearing and alerted the clerk she'd need a continuation.

She answered dozens of other incoming texts, including those from Charlie Grace and Lila. She also had missed calls from all three of her girlfriends.

Their support meant the world to her. Thick or thin...the four of them were always there for each other.

Minutes drug into hours while Reva sat in the hospital waiting room chair drinking mediocre coffee and hoping for news. "What is taking so long?" she thought, as she listened to a constant hum of distant conversations, pierced with the occasional stern voice coming over the PA. "Paging Dr. Mickelson. Paging Dr. Mickelson."

Feeling impatient, she stood and paced the linoleum floor. The scent of antiseptic cleaner lingered in the air, a reminder of the environment's purpose for health and healing. Now and then, the sliding doors swished open, admitting new arrivals.

Finally, a woman with a stethoscope draped around her neck entered from behind two automated doors at the end of the hallway. As she saw Reva's worried face, her expression turned sympathetic. "Mayor Nygard?"

Reva popped up from her seat. "Yes?"

"It looks like the little boy suffered no life-threatening internal injuries. Beyond a bruised spleen, he's remarkably unscathed." She paused, letting the information sink in. "He did sustain some blows that left soft tissue swelling and a rather large hematoma on his left leg. Again, none of this appears serious, but the medical team is recommending he remain in the hospital overnight for observation. These little ones are fragile. Better safe than sorry."

Reva's hand went to her throat. "Can I see him?"

The nurse held up a clipboard and nodded. "I'm sure that's no problem. Now, I'll need a main contact person from his immediate family. That would be you?"

Reva shook her head and explained the situation.

"Oh, yes. Mrs. Greene explained earlier. I'll call her now and ask her to come back down."

Minutes later, Mrs. Greene reappeared, the lines in her face deep and haggard. "I'm afraid, at this juncture, we've been unable to locate any family. We did trace down some basic information. The young couple was from Texas and were on their way to Yellowstone for a vacation. We tracked down the little boy's birth certificate. He was born in a Fort Worth hospital eighteen months ago. An only child. His name is Lucan Dorsey."

Reva whispered the name. It fit him.

She pulled the pen from the nurse's fingers and filled out her name and cell number. When finished, she handed the clipboard and pen back. "I'm not leaving."

The nurse smiled. "Of course. We'll add your cell to our system. In the meantime, let me lead you back so you can see him."

Navigating the logistical hurdles took several more hours, but finally, Lucan was assigned a room. The small medical center lacked a dedicated pediatric section, leading Reva to stop at the nurses' station for directions. After a brief consultation, she was guided to the third floor.

At the corridor's end, Reva heaved open a hefty door and was greeted by a nurse who was entertaining Lucan with her stethoscope. Enclosed by the crib-like bars of his small hospital bed, Lucan seemed momentarily ensnared in a world that looked a little like a prison, far removed from childhood innocence.

Upon noticing Reva, his expression transformed, eyes sparkling with recognition. She hastened to his side, her glance toward the young nurse carrying a multitude of unspoken inquiries.

"It's okay. You can pick him up," the nurse told her with an affirming nod.

Reva's initial hesitation dissolved. With a gentle yet assured motion, she lifted Lucan from the confines of his bed, embracing her role as his immediate protector in this unfamiliar environment.

"Can I have a dinner tray brought up?" the nurse offered.

"Thank you. I'd appreciate that." No way was she leaving, not even to fill her growling stomach.

As soon as the nurse vacated the room, Reva folded into the empty rocking chair. "Well, Lucan. It's just us."

With small hands, he reached into the air, grasping for something—perhaps a blanket or a familiar toy that carried the lingering scent of home. "Ma-ma," he said, looking around, his tiny voice hopeful.

Reva's heart squeezed. "Reva," she quietly said, tears streaming down her face.

She did her best to distract him, playing games with his toes and making animal sounds that brought a smile to his dimpled face. He looked at her with large, round chocolate-brown eyes.

"Everything is going to be okay," she promised again.

Over the past hours, he'd been subjected to unfamiliar faces and places that would scare even the bravest children. Now, Lucan oscillated between a desperate need for closeness and a bewildered withdrawal, a tiny soul adrift in confusion. Finally, he tired and leaned his body against hers, letting sleep overtake him, his slumber fractured by restless movements and soft whimpers.

The nurse came back into the room and offered the tray. Reva quietly told her to put it on the adjustable bedside table, then waited for the nurse to depart before laying her head against the top of Lucan's.

She was starving but nothing would make her move this sleeping baby.

The warmth of his body seeped into her own as Reva's thoughts inevitably drifted to his mother, a woman she had never met but whose presence loomed large in this moment of profound sorrow. She pondered the dreams and aspirations the young mother must have had for her child, the plans laid out for a future now irrevocably altered.

Reva imagined the countless tender moments between

mother and son, now memories that Lucan was too young to hold onto.

She thought about the love that had once surrounded the little boy, a love that had been his shield against the world. With each passing second, Reva felt a growing resolve to honor that love, to ensure that the warmth and care his mother had enveloped him with would continue, even in her absence.

In a silent vow made in the quiet of her heart, she determined to protect and cherish the fragile life left in the wake of an unimaginable loss.

At least while he was in her care until his family was found.

12

The medical team released Lucan the following morning. After completing more paperwork, Reva was assigned to be the orphaned toddler's temporary guardian, under the supervision of Child and Family Services.

At the helm of the agency was a woman who would serve as their caseworker. Shaped by years of dedicated service, Bea Followill's very presence commanded respect. The depth of understanding and compassion reflected in her eyes hinted at countless stories and decisions she had navigated with a steadfast heart. Yet, beneath her composed exterior lay a tangible weariness, a signal of the weight of her responsibilities as she stood as guardian for society's most vulnerable, their children.

Reva carried Lucan to her car and Bea instructed her on how to properly use the car seat. She'd never used one before, so the help was appreciated.

"I'll check in soon," Bea promised, handing her a bag filled with diapers and baby food.

Reva thanked her and climbed into her car, quickly glancing in the rearview mirror at Lucan who was fastened securely in a car seat in the back. Through her open window, she gave a wave to the woman seeing her off. "Thank you, Bea. I appreciate everything you've done."

"Oh, honey. You're the one who should be commended here. It is a good thing you are doing."

Reva pulled from the hospital parking lot hoping she was right. The idea of doing anything else had never crossed her mind. Still, what did she know about taking care of a baby? The occasional babysitting for Charlie Grace and Lila didn't exactly qualify her for caring for a child full-time.

She reminded herself this unexpected situation was temporary.

The idea both relieved and depressed her as memories of his soft, dark skin brought a smile to her face. Lucan was the most adorable little guy she'd ever seen. His beautiful black hair and dimpled cheeks qualified him as a poster child for cute. Those chocolate eyes, framed by long, delicate lashes, held a depth of pure wonder. He captured the hearts of everyone around him.

Reva took the long way home, avoiding driving past the accident scene. Everything would be cleaned up by now, but the site would always be a reminder of Lucan's dreadful loss. She prayed God would protect him in the years ahead as he learned the details of that fateful day.

Until then, she would do everything in her power to bring smiles to his face.

She wondered what he liked to eat. Did he have a favorite bedtime routine? Did he love to take a bath?

The gravity of the journey ahead hit her. She knew he lost his parents. She knew his age and name. That was it.

She might as well climb on a boat and try to cross the vast waters of Jenny Lake without any oars.

Reva gripped the steering wheel a little tighter and drew a deep breath. She was smart, more than capable, and had done much harder things. She'd simply have to marshal her thoughts with the precision and clarity that had always guided her endeavors.

In her mind's eye, she began to enumerate the necessities for taking care of the little orphaned toddler who had unexpectedly entered her life. First, a crib, soft and secure, where Lucan's dreams could be cradled in the warmth of safety. Then, clothes—tiny, yet essential. She'd need daytime apparel and pajamas. Nutritious food followed, alongside an array of toys and books to stimulate a young, burgeoning mind. Diapers, countless diapers, for practicality's sake.

Most of all, the little boy would need patience, love, bedtime stories whispered in the night, and a gentle, reassuring embrace to quell the nightmares. Each item, each task she mentally listed, was a brick in the foundation she was preparing to lay for this child's future—no matter how long he was in her care.

Reva, ever the planner, found herself recalibrating everything to include this new and awesome responsibility. Thank goodness she had the flexibility of taking him to work with her.

Of all her achievements, none mattered more than stepping up completely for this moment in time. The precious little boy in the back seat needed her. She was determined to rise to the occasion with all the strength and dedication she possessed.

Reva slowed her Escalade, looking in her side mirrors with extra caution, and turned onto the winding lane leading to her riverside home. She rounded the final bend and several familiar cars came into sight.

She brought her vehicle to a stop and her front door opened. Charlie Grace, Lila, and Capri poured through the entry and headed to greet her.

Reva barely climbed from her car when her friends rushed to her, enfolding her in their arms with the solemnity of support. Charlie Grace was the first to step back. "We heard about what happened, Reva. We're here for you...and for that little boy."

They waited for her to retrieve her tiny passenger from the back seat. "He's gorgeous," Lila exclaimed.

"What a doll!" Capri reached for his face, then pulled back. "Is he okay? I mean, well...you know what I mean."

Reva nodded and carried him inside, her friends following on her heels. "Time will tell. I'm sure he's traumatized." She filled them in on the few details she'd learned—his name, age, and that Family and Child Services was searching for relatives.

Charlie Grace pointed to a stack of gently used children's books and a few toys on the kitchen counter. "We didn't know what you might need, but we thought these might help him... help you both find some comfort." They all nodded.

Reva had to credit her friends for realizing she was traumatized as well. Visions of that mangled car and the impact would haunt her for some time.

Lila, always the practical one, held out a list. "I made a list of things you might need, Reva. Groceries, clothes for Lucan, anything really. We can go get them."

Reva, overwhelmed by their kindness, managed a weak smile as she lowered Lucan to the ground, watching him curiously eye the toys Charlie Grace had placed on a blanket. "I...I don't know what to say. I wasn't prepared for any of this. His parents..." Her voice broke, the grief of Lucan's loss becoming her own.

"It's okay, Reva. You don't have to say anything," Capri said, moving closer to wrap an arm around her. "We're here to help you through this. It's going to be tough, but you're not alone."

Lila knelt down to Lucan's level, offering him a toy car from the pile. "Hey there, little guy. Want to play with this?"

Lucan's gaze shifted from the toy to the faces around him, a silent pondering in his eyes before he reached out to take the car, a small gesture towards acceptance.

Reva watched, her heart aching yet warmed by the solidarity of her friends. "I'm scared," she confessed, her voice barely above a whisper. "This time I may have bitten off more than I can chew. I've never cared for a child of any age, let alone one under two years old. But having you all here...it makes it feel possible. Thank you."

Charlie Grace let out a snort. "Well, if Gibbs and Lizzy can care for a child, you can," she remarked, her eyes crinkling at the corners with laughter.

Capri elbowed her. "Let's be helpful."

Lila headed for the kitchen counter. "The authorities will make contact with his family soon. In the meantime, we'll figure this out together," Lila assured, placing the list on the expensive marble top. "I remember those early days after bringing Camille home—and the sleepless nights. Hopefully, Lucan is old enough he's sleeping more than three hours at a time." She gave Reva a weak smile.

As the morning wore on, Reva's house filled with quiet acts of love and support. Through simple dialogue and shared silences, they wove a net of care around Reva and Lucan, promising in unspoken vows to be there through the journey ahead, no matter how uncertain it seemed.

13

Reva woke with a start in her rocking chair, her arms heavy and stiff. It took several seconds for her to come fully awake and realize she was holding a sleeping little boy.

Reality flooded her mind as she relived the events of the prior days, the tragedy, and all that had unfolded since. The overwhelming responsibility weighed heavy, yet a tiny thrill bloomed inside her as she felt Lucan's heartbeat against her chest.

As she leaned into the tousled, tight curls of the toddler cradled in her arms, a gentle aroma enveloped her—a scent reminiscent of cotton sheets left to bask in the sun's embrace on her mamaw's outdoor line, subtly laced with the delicate smell of baby shampoo. The fragrance carved a sweet imprint upon her senses, a moment so serene she wished to remain forever suspended in its embrace.

The tranquility was abruptly pierced by the buzz of her phone, a jarring intrusion that startled not just her but also Lucan. She quickly fished the phone from her pocket, bracing for his cry. Instead, his face broke into a wide, infectious grin.

In an instant, Lucan's tiny head pivoted, his gaze sweeping the room with a palpable blend of innocence and curiosity. "Ma-ma?" he voiced softly, the single word striking her with the force of a bullet to the heart. "Ma-Ma?" he repeated.

The shrill tone of her phone pierced the air again. With a reluctant sigh, she answered, her voice barely above a whisper, torn between the immediacy of the call and the profound empathy she felt for Lucan as he looked for his mother.

"Hello?"

"Reva, it's Bea Followill. We've had some developments in the search for Lucan's relatives. Could you come to Child and Family Services at ten this morning? I believe you already have the address."

Reva went on high alert. They'd found his family. "Yes, of course, I'll be there."

She hung up. Melancholy immediately seeped inside. Unnerved, she pushed the unwelcome emotion aside. She was happy Lucan's family had been located.

Wasn't she?

Lucan placed his dimpled fingers against her cheek. Reva swallowed as an unbidden tear formed.

While she was happy they'd found his family, she'd secretly wished for a little more time with him.

Now, Reva stood at the threshold of goodbye, her heart a battleground of conflicting emotions. As she stood to change his diaper and get him dressed, she kissed the top of his head. "You have a big adventure ahead, little guy," she said, pushing the lump from her throat.

She laid him on her bed and unsnapped his bunny pajamas watching with a smile as the orphaned child played with his toes. She'd known this moment would come, yet she hadn't allowed herself to measure the depth of her attachment, nor had she confronted the latent desire within her to be a mother.

The phone rang yet again. Reva juggled keeping Lucan in

place long enough to dress him while bringing the phone into view. It was Charlie Grace.

"Morning," she said. "How'd the first night go?"

"Good, it went fine," she told her friend. "I'm dressing him now—or trying to. We have a meeting with Mrs. Followill later this morning."

"Yeah?"

Reva slipped the adhesive tab securely in place on his fresh diaper, proud of herself that the process had gone more smoothly than the first time she'd tried. "Yeah, sounds like they've located his extended family."

"Wow, that was quick. Of course, you can find anyone on the internet in a matter of minutes these days."

"I suppose." She reached for Lucan's pants.

"Okay, I hear something in your voice. What is it?" Charlie Grace waited on the other end of the phone for an answer, yet Reva didn't know what to say.

The years had passed so quickly. She'd always told herself she had plenty of time. Yet, here she was, at a juncture in her life where the paths of romance and parenthood seemed not just distant but possibly unreachable, a realization that carved a hollow space within her.

"It's nothing," she said, carefully trying to hide her true emotions.

"Reva?"

She tugged one leg of the pants into place. "Yeah?"

"It's going to be okay."

Somehow Charlie Grace could sense the unspoken turmoil swirling within Reva, the kind of intuitive understanding that comes from years of friendship. The reassurance in her friend's voice was like a lifeline thrown across a sea of doubt and fears.

"It's just that—" Reva began, her voice faltering as she attempted to articulate feelings she'd long kept at bay. "I guess I never realized how much I wanted...more. Until now, with

Lucan, it's like he's opened a door I can't close." She finished adjusting Lucan's pants, her actions automatic as her focus drifted to the weight of her confession.

Charlie Grace remained silent for a moment, allowing Reva's admission to settle. "I know," she finally said, her voice soft yet filled with conviction. "And it's okay to feel that way. But we both know life has a funny way of surprising us. Realizing this is what you want, but you can't see the way forward, doesn't mean the path isn't there."

Reva held the phone a little closer, drawing comfort from her friend's words. In the background, Lucan's laughter filled the room once more as he wriggled on the bed, a bittersweet reminder of the joy and complexity of these new emotions she was grappling with.

"Thank you," she whispered, a mix of gratitude and newfound resolve stirring within her. Maybe Charlie Grace was right. Now that she knew more firmly that this piece of herself —the joy of motherhood—was missing...well, maybe, just maybe, the future held possibilities she had yet to imagine.

They exchanged farewells, and Reva hung up. She tucked her phone back in her pocket and glanced at the clock on the bedside table. She'd have to hurry if she wanted time for a cup of coffee before they had to get on the road.

She picked up Lucan's tiny foot and kissed his toes. He giggled and flipped over, scrambling across her bed with the speed of a lightning bolt, his laughter filling the room.

Reva watched, a smile breaking through her sadness, as Lucan transformed her quiet bedroom into a playground of giggles and boundless energy.

Lucan's reunification with his extended family was a fitting conclusion to his story of loss—a resolution his late parents would have wanted. It was the happy ending his story deserved.

Yet, as she'd told Charlie Grace, within this celebratory milestone, a contrasting emotion had taken root in Reva's heart.

As the shadow of imminent departure loomed, this moment, with Lucan's joyous abandon echoing around her, was a poignant snapshot of what she was about to lose.

In the few hours she'd cared for him, Lucan had etched an indelible mark on her heart.

She didn't want to say goodbye.

14

The morning sun barely crept through the dust-coated windows of Thunder Mountain's decades-old veterinary office. The sign above the door, faded by years of relentless sun and wind, declared, "Tillman Strode, DVM," with the word 'DVM' nearly illegible.

The inside smelled of antiseptic, mingled with the musky odor of animals long treated and gone. The waiting room was a hodgepodge of mismatched chairs and outdated magazines, and a single, flickering fluorescent light buzzed overhead.

Lila, her chestnut brown hair pulled back in a practical ponytail, moved with purpose through the cramped, cluttered space that served as the clinic's treatment area. The room—a veritable museum of veterinary medicine—was filled with equipment and shelves lined with jars of unidentifiable specimens floating in formaldehyde.

At the center of it all was Doc Tillman, a man whose age seemed as indeterminate as the contents of those jars, yet whose presence was as commanding as ever.

"Make sure you're not wasting those supplies," Doc Tillman barked, his eyes squinting as he peered over a pair of spectacles precariously perched on the bridge of his nose. "Every penny counts in this place, Lila. Veterinary services are a unique combination of science and business. Neglect either, and the other side suffers."

"Of course, Doc," Lila responded, her voice betraying none of the frustration she felt. She was measuring out medication for a sheep with more precision than she thought necessary, but she had learned early on that arguing with Doc Tillman was a futile endeavor.

"And don't forget to update the inventory," he continued, not even looking up from the dog he was examining. "I don't want to go to the cupboard only to learn we're out of albendazole and can't treat an animal for parasites."

A small sigh escaped Lila's lips as she nodded, scribbling a note to herself. "Will do, Doc. Anything else?"

Doc Tillman finally looked up, his gaze sharp. "Yes, actually. After you're done here, the Henderson's mare is due for a check-up. They called this morning worried sick about her. I think you should go out with me and pay attention. You can't learn everything in those fancy schools, and I won't always be around to hold your hand." Then, for good measure, he added, "There's nothing on that computer I can't teach you with my hands tied behind my back."

The words stung, though Lila had learned to anticipate them. Doc Tillman had given her a rare chance when offering her a job way back in high school—a job she'd moved on from when she married and was following her husband around the country as a military wife.

When Aaron was killed, and she had a sudden need for income, Doc created a position and brought her back on full-time, a move she strongly suspected was motivated more by the grouchy old veterinarian's generosity than need.

. . .

Doc Tillman snorted, turning back to his work. He attached a plastic cone around the dog's neck, picked up the animal, and put him in a nearby cage. "Just remember where you are. Thunder Mountain isn't exactly the big city. We do things differently here."

Lila forced a smile, though her heart sometimes grew heavy. She knew her worth, or at least she wanted to believe she did. Yet, in the shadow of Doc Tillman's towering ego and the outmoded wooden-paneled walls of the vet office, it was hard to remember.

She silently vowed to prove herself, not just to Doc Tillman but to the entire town of Thunder Mountain. But deep down, she feared that no matter how much she learned or how hard she worked, it would never be enough for Doc Tillman.

That thought was a heavy chain around her spirit, one she wasn't sure how to break.

The delicate chime of a small bell resonated through the room as the door swung open. Lila cast her gaze toward the modest waiting area, catching a glimpse of the new arrival through the doorway. "I'll go see who it is," she offered, moving towards the front.

Earl Dunlop, a large, gruff man who ran the county snow removal fleet, stepped inside, cradling a ginger-colored kitty in his arms—a sight so incongruous it could have softened even the hardest of hearts.

"I need some help here," Earl announced in a voice that was filled with concern as he made his way to the front counter.

Doc Tillman followed Lila, his eyebrows knitting together in curiosity. "What seems to be the trouble?" he asked, his tone carrying the weight of years spent diagnosing and treating all manners of animal ailments.

Earl shifted uncomfortably, the kitty's soft mewling barely audible. "Well, Doc. I think Fluffy's got a bad case of urinary tract infection. Been noticing her straining to pee, and she's been quite off lately."

Doc Tillman's eyebrows shot up in surprise. "What bull dropped that on the floor?" he exclaimed, a mixture of amusement and skepticism in his voice. The phrase was one of his favorites.

Doc followed Earl's gaze at Lila with suspicion. "Figures," Doc Tillman muttered under his breath.

He straightened and glanced between them. "Listen up. More often than not, straining to urinate is a signal related to kidney stones or blockages."

The color seemed to drain from Earl's face. "Sounds bad." He looked over at Lila, searching for a sympathetic audience. Lila, who had been observing the exchange quietly, offered him a reassuring smile, understanding the worry that drove him to bring his pet to the vet's office.

Doc Tillman reached for the cat. "Here, give Fluffy to me. We'll do a few tests and get her all fixed up. I promise." Despite his stern expression, it was clear he had a soft spot for the animals and their owners who sought his help.

Earl carefully handed the kitty over, whispering soothing words to calm the frightened animal.

Lila was about to suggest Earl grab some breakfast at the Rustic Pine when Doc Tillman, cat securely in tow, halted at the doorway to the back. He threw a quick look over his shoulder, his expression steeped in impatience. "Coming? Or is the cat diagnosing itself today?"

15

Reva's heart weighed heavy with a bittersweet burden as she walked across the parking lot of Family and Child Services. In her arms, eighteen-month-old Lucan remained blissfully unaware of the gravity of the day and the changes that lay ahead.

Reva had embraced this unexpected and temporary role with a mix of dedication and apprehension. Even in the short time she'd cared for him, Lucan had opened a part of her heart she hadn't realized was longing to be filled.

Now, standing before the building where she would have to say goodbye, she was torn between relief that Lucan might have family to take him in and sadness at the thought of letting him go.

Reva stepped into the starkly lit lobby of the Family and Child Services building, her boots echoing on the polished floor as she crossed to the reception desk. "I'm Reva Nygard. I'm here to see Bea Followill."

The clerk nodded. "Yes, Ms. Followill is expecting you."

As Reva stood, clutching Lucan a little closer, she saw Bea Followill approaching through the lobby.

"Reva, thank you for coming on such short notice," she said, with a calm demeanor and a compassionate smile that eased some of Reva's apprehension. Dressed in a simple professional blouse and slacks, Bea exuded an air of practicality and warmth, the kind of person you find yourself confiding in without reservation. As she drew nearer, her expression conveyed a mixture of understanding and sadness, a silent acknowledgment of the complex emotions Reva was grappling with.

"I understand this is hard for you," Bea continued, leading them to her tiny office. "Thank you so very much for stepping up after the accident and taking care of this little one." She tweaked his dimpled cheek.

"So, you have news?" Reva prompted as she took a seat and unwrapped Lucan from his jacket. "Family willing to take him in?" Her voice remained steady despite the turmoil she felt inside.

Bea folded into her office chair and let out a sigh—a long, heavy sound that seemed to carry more weight than the air could hold. "We did find a relative...his grandfather. But—" She paused, searching Reva's eyes. "Jess Dorsey is currently serving time in Texas for armed robbery. Until we can ensure Lucan's safety and find a more permanent solution, we're at a bit of a standstill."

"I—I'm not following."

"Technically, Lucan's grandfather is his legal guardian until he relinquishes or the courts rule otherwise. Either way, that process will take time. We've notified Mr. Dorsey about the accident and hope to assess his intent to care for his grandson after his release. He has about nine months left to serve out his sentence."

Reva scowled with concern. "He's a criminal," she protested. "I mean, is he the best one to care for Lucan? There's no other family?"

"I'm afraid there's no one but Mr. Dorsey." Bea looked across the desk patiently. "Given the current situation, we need a more long-term solution. Nothing permanent at this point. We have no choice but to secure foster care for Lucan."

Bea folded her hands on her desk. "Reva, I know this is a lot to ask, but would you consider keeping Lucan a bit longer? Only until we find a suitable foster family or another solution," Bea implored, her eyes pleading.

The room seemed to spin as Reva processed Bea's words. She thought of the hours she'd spent holding Lucan through the night, comforting him, and the surprising amount of love she already felt for this little guy in her lap.

The possibility of handing Lucan over to a distant, incarcerated relative was unthinkable. Yet, the alternative—keeping Lucan—meant altering her life in ways she'd never imagined.

"Bea, I'm single, I'm the mayor, my life is...it's not designed for this." Reva tried to articulate the storm of objections in her mind, but each quickly dissipated, sounding less convincing than the last.

"I understand your reservations, Reva. But you're all he has right now. And you've been doing an amazing job. If it's too much, I will find him a foster family. I promise," Bea said, her sincerity unmistakable.

The silence that followed was filled with unspoken fears and hopes. Reva felt a tug at her heart, a call to a purpose she hadn't planned for but suddenly couldn't imagine abandoning.

Bea was right. She was all he had, and perhaps, he was what she didn't know she needed.

She let her lips drop to the top of his soft, black curls and kissed him. He turned and looked up at her, his large, brown eyes filled with nothing but trust.

"Okay," Reva finally said, her voice a mixture of resolve and wonder. "I'll keep him. Until there's a better plan. He..." She swallowed the lump forming in her throat. "Lucan has already become a part of my life. How can I say no?"

Bea's relief was palpable. "Thank you, Reva. I can't tell you how much this means. We'll support you every step of the way."

As Reva made her way to the car, cradling Lucan, the gravity of her choice settled on her shoulders. It was a commitment that would change her life, but looking into Lucan's eyes, she knew it was the right one.

There was no way to know what lay ahead or how long Lucan would be with her. Still, in her heart, she knew she'd care for this precious baby boy for as long as God allowed.

With renewed determination, she adjusted him in her arms, basking in the sky-blue morning stretching out above them. The road ahead would be uncertain, but they would navigate it together, a newfound family forged from tragedy and love.

"Well, little man, it looks like it's you and me against the world." Reva reached and wiped a tear from the corner of her eye. "Let's go home."

16

The early afternoon sun pierced the dense canopy of towering pines creating a mesmerizing, dappled effect on the pavement as Reva navigated the winding road on her way home.

Her appointment at Child and Family Services had been emotionally draining. She sped up a little, eager to kick off her heels and settle down in a familiar setting where she could wrap her head around what had transpired. Besides that, she hadn't planned on bringing him home with her, so hadn't packed any food or extra diapers. Lucan had to be hungry.

Reva cast a glance at her little guy in the rearview mirror. You wouldn't know it from the smile on his face. Lucan was such a happy baby, especially given all he'd been through. Since the accident, he'd been shuffled into strangers' hands, slept in an unfamiliar place, and was palpably aware his mommy and daddy were missing. Most toddlers would have a complete meltdown over much less.

Still, she didn't want to push her good fortune. She needed to get this sweet-natured toddler home, feed him, and get him settled down for a nap. Then, she would deal with the mountain of items that demanded her attention and all the looming changes to her schedule.

In the back, Lucan's lip quivered, and he began fussing. She'd spoken too soon, it seemed.

"I know, sweetie. We'll be home soon." She turned on the radio and shuffled through the stations until a lively tune blasted through the speakers. She sang along, hoping to distract him.

Thankfully, the strategy worked. Lucan grew wide-eyed and bobbed his little head up and down to the beat of the tune. He seemed to enjoy music!

Reva rounded a bend. Per her mental calculation, they'd be home in less than a half hour.

Suddenly, the car jolted. The tranquility of the drive was shattered by the unmistakable thud and drag of a flat tire.

Muttering under her breath, Reva pulled over to the side of the remote road, her car coming to a halt amidst a stand of aspen trees mingled in the pines. She turned the music off and reluctantly opened the car door.

Stepping out in her heels, Reva assessed the situation.

The flat tire mocked her.

"Why now?" she cried out, her frustration echoing against the backdrop of the silent trees. She could call someone but that would take time.

She had no choice but to slip off her heels and deal with the situation.

Reva opened the back passenger door. "I'll be right back, sweetheart."

She moved to the rear of the vehicle where she opened the powered rear liftgate and rummaged through the trunk compartment for the spare and jack.

Inside the car, Lucan began to cry.

Reva dropped the tire and jack on the ground and quickly moved for the open back door, leaned in, and tried to quiet the fussy child. When the effort proved fruitless, she picked through the bag she'd packed, looking for anything edible.

Nothing.

Groaning, she realized that the only thing she had was a pack of gum in her purse. There was also not one single diaper.

What had she been thinking?

Her head moved in a disbelieving shake, frustration mounting as the full scope of her predicament became apparent. She left for her meeting believing Lucan would remain with Bea, that's what. When she'd packed a travel bag, she'd never imagined returning with Lucan in tow and needing more supplies.

Lucan's cries escalated, a stark reminder of his hunger and discomfort.

Reva plucked him from his car seat and tried to soothe him. His cries only grew louder.

A commotion in the trees pulled her attention, followed by a low growl.

From the corner of her eye, she spotted a bear and its cubs emerging from the trees, their curious eyes fixed on her and Lucan.

Panic surged through Reva's veins. She had no bear spray, no protection.

With her heart pounding in terror, she scrambled back into the car and slammed the door closed, clutching Lucan close as she prayed for the bear to lose interest and wander past despite Lucan's loud wails.

With trembling fingers, she reached for the button and closed the power lift door.

The moments stretched into eternity as the bear and its cubs lingered, exploring the side of her shiny black Escalade. Reva's breaths came in short, sharp gasps, her eyes fixed on the massive form just yards away.

Inches away from the glass, the black bear's features were

strikingly detailed and formidable. Its fur was dense, shimmering, deep black. Eyes, deep-set and inquisitive. The prominent snout twitched subtly, sniffing out potential threats. Rounded ears sat atop its head, moving with keen alertness as Lucan's cries continued.

The sheer bulk of the bear, visible through the barrier of the car window, served as a vivid reminder of its strength and agility, igniting a primal fear deep inside Reva as she held her breath and clutched Lucan tightly against her chest.

She slowly reached inside her bag and pulled out her phone only to learn she had no bars. That meant no service.

Just as despair began to set in, the sound of an engine broke the tense silence.

An old green pickup rolled to a stop behind the car. The person inside seemed to assess her predicament and laid on the horn, long and loud.

The mama bear reared up, her ears alert. Just as quickly, she turned and pounded the pavement, pushing her cubs along and back into the safety of the trees.

Reva sighed with relief, her eyes immediately brimming with tears as the treacherous moment passed.

Why hadn't she thought to honk her horn?

The driver's door opened on the old pickup and out climbed a man. Not just any man, but the same black man she'd met on the hiking trail a few days ago. His appearance was a beacon of hope in her moment of desperation.

Recognition flickered in his eyes as he assessed the scene—a woman, overwhelmed and scared, a baby crying in her arms, and a family of bears retreating into the trees.

With a calmness that belied the situation, he approached. His golden retriever followed at his heels. "Hey, there. You okay?"

Reva swallowed and reluctantly nodded. "Yeah. We're fine."

"I believe we met earlier—on the trail? I'm Kellen Warner."

Without waiting for her answer, he reached for Lucan. "You mind?"

Reva consented with a shake of her head.

Kellen extracted the crying toddler from her embrace, quieting Lucan by jiggling him on his hip.

"I'm afraid he's hungry," she confessed, her voice carrying a hint of vulnerability.

"No problem, we'll take care of that." He motioned for her to follow him back to his truck, where he retrieved an old metal lunchbox from the bed of the vehicle. He pulled a banana from inside and handed it to her, grinning. "Sorry, my hands are a bit full."

Grateful, she flashed him a warm smile, carefully peeling the banana. "Thank you," she expressed, gently placing a slice into Lucan's eager, dimpled hand. The little boy's face lit up with joy as he eagerly munched on the offered snack.

Kellen watched with a pleased smile, then handed Lucan back to Reva and turned his attention to the flat tire. "Now, let's see to getting this fixed." He glanced down at her bare feet and smiled.

Kellen worked swiftly, his hands skillfully maneuvering the tools to replace the flat tire. Reva watched him, the warmth of gratitude mixing with a budding sense of curiosity about the man who had appeared so serendipitously in her moment of need. She couldn't help but notice the confident, methodical way his hands moved, silent evidence of his capability and care. There was a gentle ease in his presence, a strength that felt reassuring.

Once the tire was securely in place, Kellen wiped his hands on a rag, his gaze meeting Reva's. "There, all set," he announced, his voice carrying a hint of satisfaction. "Make sure to get that tire looked at when you can."

"Thank you," Reva replied, her voice softer than she

intended. "I don't know what I would have done without your help today."

"It was nothing," Kellen said, but his smile suggested he was glad to have been there for her. "Just happy I could help."

There was a brief pause, a moment suspended in time where possibilities seemed to hover in the air between them. "Maybe I could repay you somehow? Coffee, sometime?" Reva ventured, surprised by her own boldness.

Kellen's smile widened and he nodded. "Sure. I'd like that," he said, his eyes holding hers in a look that promised more than just a casual meeting. He dug inside his flannel shirt pocket, pulled out a business card, and handed it to her.

As he climbed back into his truck, Reva felt a flicker of excitement, a stirring of hope. Perhaps this chance encounter was the beginning of something new, one more chapter in her life she hadn't dared to anticipate. Watching the truck drive away, she felt Lucan's weight in her arms and smiled down at him, filled with a renewed sense of optimism.

Life had a way of surprising her—just when she thought she understood how things stood, everything shifted, upending her expectations. Yet, in the quiet aftermath of the day's unexpected turns, Reva realized that change, with all its uncertainties, was also the bearer of new beginnings.

17

"Thank you, Ernie." Reva balanced Lucan on her hip as she stood in the center of her office. "Your help with assembling the crib is so appreciated."

Ernie tucked his screwdriver into his back pocket, his smile broad. "It was no trouble at all. I already had the tools I needed at the shop. I'm glad to lend a hand."

Verna Billingsley struck a hands-on-hips pose. "I don't see how you expect to get anything done with a toddler in your office," she remarked, shaking her head with skepticism. "And just so you're aware, babysitting isn't my forte."

Reva offered her a calm smile. "Duly noted. But I'm planning to work half-days for now, until we find our rhythm." She gently kissed the little boy's forehead. "Right, Lucan?"

Verna remained unconvinced. "And don't count on me for any of those *Zoomer* calls. I keep my distance from all that tech nonsense," she declared.

This brought a chuckle from Ernie.

Verna scowled back at him. "What? You don't know any more than I do about those things."

Reva chose not to engage with Verna's reluctance, understanding that her assistant's aversion often stemmed from fear of the unknown. She understood. The challenges of adapting to new circumstances could be daunting, as she was now learning.

"Let's see how this goes," Reva murmured, gently placing Lucan into the crib. It was then she noticed a milk stain marring the lapel of her black suit jacket.

Without missing a beat, Verna produced a handkerchief from her bra, quickly moistening it with water from a glass on Reva's desk, and began dabbing at the stain. "When does the memorial start?" she asked.

Casting a quick glance at the wall clock, Reva replied, "We have less than an hour. I'd better hurry." She expressed her gratitude to Verna, silently reminding herself to dispose of the water to avoid accidentally drinking it later.

Verna, always one step ahead, picked up the glass and gestured for Ernie to follow her towards the door.

Ernie paused. "It was incredibly kind of you to organize this memorial for the little one's parents." He shook his head solemnly. "It's a truly heartbreaking situation."

Reva offered a somber nod. "It was something I had to do. They didn't have anyone else."

She had wrestled with the decision of whether to bring Lucan to the cemetery. Ultimately, she concluded that, although he was too young to retain any memory of it, there would come a day when he would find comfort in knowing he had been there. Moreover, she felt confident that his parents would have cherished the thought of their little boy attending their farewell service.

As they stepped from the car later that morning into the bright sunny day, Reva reflected on the fragile thread by which life hangs, marveling at how swiftly everything can shift—for both good and bad. Sometimes at the same time. That young

mother's loss had become the possibility of her unspoken dream being fulfilled. It was a humbling thought, the realization that joy and sorrow can often be two sides of the same coin.

The cemetery, a tranquil haven nestled in the heart of towering pines, exuded a serene beauty. The air was filled with the crisp scent of pine, mingling with the earthy fragrance of the surrounding forest. The lawn, a sprawling expanse of lush green, was meticulously manicured, evidencing the community's reverence for this sacred place.

The graves, each marked by tombstones that ranged from simple, weathered stones to more elaborate memorials, were carefully lined up throughout the cemetery. These stones, etched with the names and dates of those who had passed, stood as silent testimonials to lives intertwined with the fabric of the town. Reva, as she moved among them, felt a profound connection to almost every name. These were not just markers of those who had gone before; they were reminders of stories, of laughter shared, and of hardships endured together. Each one represented a thread in the tapestry of the community's shared history, from pioneers who had settled the area to recent friends lost too soon.

Reva made her way toward the blue canvas canopy. She was taken aback by the unexpectedly large turnout, especially considering that none of the people assembled around the two elegantly crafted wooden caskets, adorned with a cascade of white roses, had ever known the Dorseys personally.

Albie Barton and Fleet Southcott stood solemnly near Clancy Rivers, who was seated in his wheelchair, each of them donned formal suits that mirrored the gravity of the occasion. Wooster and Nicola Cavendish marked their presence as well, adding to the collective show of respect. The entire Knit Wits group had also turned out in full force.

As Reva made her way into the gathering, she was warmly

welcomed by Capri, Charlie Grace, and Lila. Their familiar faces and comforting hugs enveloped her, symbolizing the unspoken support that thrived among them.

"How are you managing, honey?" Charlie Grace inquired, her voice laced with concern.

"I'm fine." Reva backed up her assertion with a firm smile.

Her friends were worried about her—a worry she wanted them to know was completely unfounded. What mattered most was Lucan.

Reva's mind was a tempest of emotions as she thought about the orphaned little boy, a tender soul left to navigate the world without the guiding hands of his parents. She couldn't help but reflect on the profound love they had for him, a love that was tragically cut short, leaving behind a silence where laughter and warmth had once resided.

The unfairness of their premature departure from this life weighed heavily on her heart, a poignant reminder of the fragility of existence. In the quiet moments of the night, she pondered the dreams and aspirations they must have harbored for their son, dreams now entrusted to her care—hopefully long-term.

It was a responsibility she felt deeply, a commitment to honor their memory by ensuring that their love continued to surround him, even in their absence. The thought of this little boy, orphaned yet surrounded by a community willing to embrace him, sparked a determination in Reva to provide him with all the love, security, and opportunities his parents would have wished for him.

While the task before her seemed daunting, she would embrace this new role and do her best to craft a legacy of love that defied the cruel twist of fate.

Annie Cumberland enveloped her in a warm, comforting embrace. "I'm so grateful you requested Pete to speak today."

Pete's contributions to Thunder Mountain went far beyond

his pastoral responsibilities at Moose Chapel. He was esteemed not just as a spiritual guide but also as a trusted confidante, an insightful counselor, and a cherished friend to both his congregation and the broader community of Thunder Mountain. Alongside his wife, Annie, Pete managed the Rustic Pine Tavern, affectionately referred to by him as his "other church."

Pastor Pete stepped forward, his presence commanding a gentle silence among the gathered mourners. Clearing his throat softly, he opened his Bible and began, "In times of sorrow, we often find ourselves searching for understanding, for a sign that there's a greater plan at work." He paused, allowing his words to resonate with the quiet assembly before continuing. "The scripture tells us in John 3:8, 'The wind blows wherever it pleases. You hear its sound, but you cannot tell where it comes from or where it is going. So it is with everyone born of the Spirit.'"

He looked around, his eyes reflecting the depth of his empathy. "Much like the unpredictable path of the wind, the sudden tragedy that called Michael and Kayla Dorsey back to their Creator reminds us of life's fragile and unfathomable nature. We may not understand the why of it all, but we can find solace in trusting their Maker, whose movements are beyond our comprehension but always purposeful. Let us remember them not for how they left this world, but for the love, joy, and spirit they contributed to it—and to the life of their son, Lucan, who remains a living testament to their legacy."

Pastor Pete's words, steeped in faith and compassion, offered a beacon of hope, likening the incomprehensible paths of life and death to the mysterious but always meaningful ways of the Spirit.

Pete gently closed his Bible, his eyes meeting Reva's. "Mayor, would you like to share a few words?"

Reva felt the weight of the moment, a deep sense of responsibility urging her to speak. Yet, when she attempted to articulate her thoughts, words eluded her.

Sensing Reva's distress, Lila gracefully intervened. Clutching a rose, she moved to stand beside Reva in a gesture of solidarity. "Let's bow our heads," she suggested softly.

"Lord, we thank You for the lives of Michael and Kayla Dorsey. We pray for Your blessings upon their little boy as he grows. Infuse his life with joy, happiness, and profound purpose. Guide Reva as she nurtures him, providing him with a loving home until You unveil Your next plan. Amen."

The prayer was followed by a chorus of amens, floating gently through the crisp mountain air, a collective whisper of faith and hope. Then, in a poignant ritual of honor, each person present approached the caskets to lay down single roses, a silent symphony of grief, love, and solidarity encapsulated in the simple yet profound act.

As the final rose was placed, Reva's gaze softened on Lucan, who had succumbed to slumber in her arms, his plump hands gripping her suit lapel with innocent trust. She inhaled deeply, fortified by the collective support of those around her.

When the service concluded, she followed the others back to their cars, carrying the sleeping child.

"It was a lovely service," someone muttered.

"Yes, it certainly was," came a soft answer.

At her car, she bid her girlfriends a quick goodbye, then bent to fasten Lucan safely in his car seat. The buckle clicked, and she checked to make sure the strap was snugly in place, then shut the door and reached for the handle on the driver's side.

The day had been hard, as expected—yet Pastor Pete's message helped put everything in perspective.

Before stepping into her car, Reva paused to take in the surrounding scenery. In the distance, the sun filtered through the pines, casting soft, golden light over the cemetery—a promise that even in the darkest times, there was hope on the horizon.

18

Reva jolted awake, feeling every ache in her bones and muscles—a testament to the night she spent in the new rocking chair cradling Lucan.

Charlie Grace had emphasized the importance of a consistent bedtime routine, yet Reva found it impossible to ignore Lucan's forlorn gaze from the crib. The idea of leaving him there, so visibly yearning for comfort, was unthinkable. She rationalized that Lucan, surely missing his parents deeply, needed the added reassurance of her embrace to drift into sleep. However, this tender ritual often led to her own unintended slumber as well.

On this particular morning, Lucan sat on her lap wide awake watching her.

"Well, good morning little punkin."

His dimpled face broke into a wide grin.

Raising a child was like witnessing the unfolding of a delicate miracle right before her eyes. Each day brought a new discovery, a fresh challenge that somehow managed to tighten the bonds of love she felt for this little guy even more.

She'd always suspected motherhood was wonderful, but

the pines, casting soft, golden light over the cemetery—a promise that even in the darkest times, there was hope on the horizon.

18

Reva jolted awake, feeling every ache in her bones and muscles—a testament to the night she spent in the new rocking chair cradling Lucan.

Charlie Grace had emphasized the importance of a consistent bedtime routine, yet Reva found it impossible to ignore Lucan's forlorn gaze from the crib. The idea of leaving him there, so visibly yearning for comfort, was unthinkable. She rationalized that Lucan, surely missing his parents deeply, needed the added reassurance of her embrace to drift into sleep. However, this tender ritual often led to her own unintended slumber as well.

On this particular morning, Lucan sat on her lap wide awake watching her.

"Well, good morning little punkin."

His dimpled face broke into a wide grin.

Raising a child was like witnessing the unfolding of a delicate miracle right before her eyes. Each day brought a new discovery, a fresh challenge that somehow managed to tighten the bonds of love she felt for this little guy even more.

She'd always suspected motherhood was wonderful, but

she had underestimated the powerful emotions that accompanied the job.

There was this indescribable joy in the simplest moments—seeing his sleepy smile first thing in the morning, hearing the uninhibited laughter that bubbled up over the smallest things, or feeling the tiny grip of his hand in hers. It was a journey of constant amazement, where the mundane became magical.

Despite the sleepless nights and the endless worries, the privilege of caring for a young life, of being their constant, their teacher, and their haven, filled Reva's heart with a love so profound it was almost overwhelming. This journey, with all its ups and downs, was a beautiful, bewildering adventure she wouldn't trade for the world.

Of course, the urgency of her other responsibilities could be a tyrant.

A swift glance at the bedside clock confirmed her fears; she was alarmingly late. So late, in fact, she decided to momentarily abandon her steadfast rule against eating outside the kitchen.

Balancing Lucan on her hip, she made her way to the kitchen, where she swiftly gathered a container of applesauce and a small plastic spoon, expertly managing them with one hand while ensuring Lucan remained snug against her with the other. Skillfully, she nudged the highchair closer with her foot and secured Lucan inside. In a feat of maternal dexterity, she lifted the highchair—toddler, applesauce, and all—and began the precarious journey upstairs. Each step was measured and cautious as she navigated the bulky chair to the master bathroom. Once there, she gently placed it on the floor and, with a sense of urgency, stripped off yesterday's blouse—yes, she had slept in her clothes, a silent testament to the chaotic beauty of this parenthood adventure.

Minutes later she stepped inside a steaming shower, feeling a sense of pride. She had this.

The thought no more than left her mind when a high-volume shriek came from the other side of the beveled-glass shower door. She jumped from the shower, not bothering to grab a towel.

The source of the little boy's displeasure became immediately apparent.

Lucan had knocked his container of applesauce off the tray and onto her expensive travertine tile—the flooring she'd ordered from Italy and had installed last year. Not only was the sticky substance splayed across the tiles, but the sauce was launched up the walls and spattered onto the counter and mirror. It looked like a baby war zone!

Her initial shock quickly morphed into a cocktail of frustration and disbelief as she surveyed the chaos that now adorned her meticulously curated bathroom. She didn't have time for this.

Breathing deeply, she tried to quell the rising tide of irritation. "Lucan," she began, her voice a mix of exasperation and forced calm, as she stepped cautiously over the gooey mess, feeling the sticky applesauce squelch underfoot.

As she knelt beside the little boy, her heart softened at the sight of his wide, apologetic eyes. The mess, while vast, paled in comparison to the innocence reflected in his gaze. "It's okay, sweetheart," she found herself saying, the annoyance dissipating as quickly as it had arrived. "Let's just get this cleaned up."

Reva hoped the morning's chaos would be the extent of her troubles for the day. Yet, upon arriving at her office, over an hour late with little Lucan accompanying her, she was met with another unforeseen complication.

"Oh, Reva. You're finally here!" Verna hurried toward her from her desk, wringing her hands. "I've been trying to reach you."

Perplexed, Reva fished her phone out of her pocket, realizing she had forgotten to reactivate its ringer after muting it the previous night to prevent disturbing Lucan's sleep. "I can't believe I missed your calls. I'm so sorry," she apologized, pressing the button to restore the sound, all while balancing her briefcase and Lucan on her opposite side.

Verna reached out and lifted Lucan from her arms, relieving her of the little boy's weight. "Let me help you with him."

With a nod of thanks, Reva proceeded towards her office.

"Actually, it's best if you don't go there," Verna interjected hesitantly.

Reva frowned, puzzled. "And why's that?"

Verna's face conveyed the gravity of the situation. "There's been a mishap. The waterline burst sometime in the middle of the night. Your office...it's underwater."

Reva's initial response was a momentary freeze, the kind that comes from utter disbelief. Her frown deepened, a mix of alarm and resignation washing over her features as she processed Verna's words. The weight of the situation momentarily anchored her in place. She let out a long, slow breath.

"Of course," Reva finally said, her voice laced with weary acceptance—a stark contrast to the shockwave that went off inside her upon hearing the news. "Why am I not surprised? It seems the universe has quite the sense of humor today."

She glanced down at Lucan, momentarily finding solace in his obliviousness to the chaos surrounding them. Then, looking back at Verna, she mustered a half-smile that didn't quite reach her eyes. "Well, no use crying over spilled water, right? Let's see the damage."

With that, Reva followed Verna, stepping with a deliberate calmness she didn't feel. Each step felt like wading through the symbolic floodwaters of her life's current state—overwhelmed, but not yet sinking. She was determined to navigate this latest challenge with the same resolve she applied to every aspect of her life.

Long ago, she'd determined to be a woman characterized by her strength, adaptability, and perseverance in the face of adversity. She had strong role models—both her mother and mamaw, God rest her soul—possessed unwavering spirits that refused to be broken, no matter the challenges or setbacks encountered.

While Reva had never experienced school segregation or the deeply ingrained cultural issues of the south, she had wrestled her demon of alcoholism, a trek that taught her the importance of acknowledging her feelings, but she also knew how to prevent them from overwhelming her.

Still, nothing could have prepared her for what she saw when Verna opened the door and she was able to survey the damage.

Reva's hand flew to her chest. "Oh, my!" For a moment, she struggled to breathe as she took in the fact that her office floor was covered in at least an inch of water. The flow streamed out into the hallway and over her favorite pair of Manolo Blahnik heels—the violet stilettos that matched her suit perfectly.

"I called the city engineer," Verna reported. "He immediately shut down the power. He's working now to get the water turned off."

The ceiling had caved directly over her desk, and soggy pieces of drywall were scattered everywhere. The water main, hidden from sight in the darkened space above the ceiling, continued to gush water, spewing all over the desk, soaking important documents and electronic devices—including Reva's laptop.

Files that once held the city's plans and projects were drenched and floating. Her computer and phone were puddled in water, potentially ruining them, and losing vital information.

The water didn't stop at the desk. It spread across the room, soaking carpets, furniture, and artwork, turning the mayor's office into a flooded mess. Staff scrambled to salvage what they could, moving items to higher ground and attempting to stem the flow of water, but the damage was immediate and extensive.

Lucan chose that moment to cry. Not a small whimper but an all-out screeching wail. Reva waded through the water and took the ill-tempered child from her assistant's arms. "Shh..." she murmured, trying to quiet him. Her attempt only served to push him into a more frenzied meltdown. He arched his back and plummeted his fists in the air, waving them wildly in a fit.

Reva glanced around, feeling helpless, as the crew all turned to stare at her and the developing situation. As she attempted to calm Lucan with a melody her grandmother once sang, her voice cracked under the strain, failing to convey the comfort she so desperately wanted to provide.

The chaos of the flooding office seemed to swallow her efforts whole, rendering them ineffective. Lucan, far from being soothed, escalated his cries, his small body writhing in frustration. The water continued its relentless spread, indifferent to the human drama unfolding.

Feeling her attempt to quiet Lucan flounder, Reva's heart sank. She glanced around, seeking a lifeline in the eyes of her staff, only to find them equally overwhelmed, their actions disjointed in the face of the disaster. The sense of failure weighed heavily on her, not just in her inability to comfort Lucan but also in her responsibility as the leader who was supposed to guide her team through crises.

Her voice faltered and finally fell silent, drowned out by the cacophony of the water's rush and Lucan's inconsolable crying.

Likewise, the flood continued its destructive path. Her iPad cord was now underwater, important documents turned into papier-mâché, and the heritage furniture that once adorned the mayor's office began to warp and swell.

The floodwaters, together with Lucan's loud cries, were

indifferent to her good intentions and laid bare the limits of her control.

The lesson was clear, though harsh—not all battles could be won with determination and a song.

19

"Hey, thanks for agreeing to meet at my house tonight," Reva told her girlfriends as she placed a large tray of finger sandwiches on the coffee table.

Charlie Grace carried a large pitcher of strawberry daiquiris into the living room. "You've had quite the few days. It's to be expected, with the major life change you just made," she remarked while filling the waiting stemmed glasses, skipping Reva's which was already brimming with her virgin mocktail. "And planning the funeral had to be a drain on your emotions."

"You don't know the half of it," Reva told her. "You will not believe the day I've had. It's like something out of a disaster movie."

Lila leaned forward with curiosity. "Oh? What happened? Was it Bill Buckley from accounting again?"

Charlie Grace shook her head with a grin. "Please tell me he finally wore matching socks."

Reva sighed and leaned back against the plush chair cushion. "I wish it were that amusing. But it's much worse. Our office flooded. And I mean, seriously flooded."

Capri's eyes widened. "Flooded? How did that happen?"

Reva kicked off her shoes. "It turns out the building's old pipes finally gave out. Water everywhere—carpets, equipment, files. You name it."

"Oh, no!" Lila's voice was filled with sympathy. "That sounds like a nightmare. What did you do?"

Reva was quick to answer. "Well, at first, I just stood there, watching my desk become an island. I mean, there were literal waves every time someone walked through the water."

Charlie Grace broke into laughter. "I'm sorry to make light of this, but I'm picturing you surfing on your office chair."

Reva smiled despite the situation. "Honestly, at one point, that seemed like a viable option. But then, panic mode kicked in. We had to salvage what we could."

Capri reached for a sandwich. "Was anything important ruined?"

"Thankfully, most of our crucial documents are backed up digitally," Reva told them. "But some of the physical files weren't so lucky. And our poor office plants drowned."

Lila's hand went to her chest in mock despair. "Not the plants! Were you able to save any?"

"A few." Reva took a sip from her glass. She smiled. "But let's have a moment of silence for the fern I've somehow kept alive for three years. It doesn't look like it'll survive the flood."

Charlie Grace grinned and held up her cocktail glass in a toast. "Here's to the great fern catastrophe. We'll remember you fondly."

"Well, if you need any help with replacing water valves, tell the guys to just give me a call. I helped fix Betty Dunning's kitchen sink last week. Her P-trap was cracked and leaking. Made the kitchen smell like rotten eggs." Capri raised the sandwich to inspect the egg salad nestled between the slices of bread.

"So, what's the plan now?" she asked casually, shrugging

before taking a bite. "Are you going to work from home?" Her words were muffled by her chewing.

Reva passed her friend a napkin, a smile playing on her lips. "Seems so. The office is closed for repairs for the next couple of weeks. Which means...pajama workdays!"

Charlie Grace rolled her eyes. "As if you'd actually work in your PJs."

Reva paused, a thoughtful expression crossing her face as she tilted her head slightly, directing her ear towards the staircase. "Do you hear that?" she asked.

All three of the women on her sofa shook their heads.

"It's nothing. Lucan is likely asleep," Capri said.

Lila nodded in agreement. "Besides, if that little guy wakes, he'll nod back off." She pointed to the baby monitor on the table. "You'll know if something needs attention," she assured.

Charlie Grace lifted the cocktail glass and took a sip. Her expression immediately turned soft. "Oh, this is good." She shifted to face Reva. "You're finding out motherhood is an extreme sport. That's why most of us moms wear workout clothes every day."

Lila nodded in agreement. "The biggest thing I remember is that there was just no transition. You had to hit the ground diapering."

"Oh, but wait. They grow up. That's when the real fun begins," Charlie Grace warned. "Before I had Jewel, I didn't know I could ruin someone's day by saying, '*Get dressed, please.*'"

They all laughed. It felt good to laugh after the week Reva had experienced. While her friends were attempting to console her, juggling motherhood—even if temporary—with her duties and responsibilities had been far more challenging than expected.

She sighed, admitting, "I just didn't realize I would have to know everything by my second rodeo. That's still a very low number of rodeos."

Lila laughed and reached for her drink. "By the time they are teenagers, it's nothing but the Wild West. Take, for example, my daughter's upcoming prom."

Charlie Grace kicked her stocking feet up on the edge of the table. "I love the dress Camille picked out. The pink color really sets off her blonde hair."

Lila sipped her daiquiri. "At least she settled on the dress. Prom date? Not so much."

"What do you mean?" Reva asked.

"Well, she wants to dump Randy Eisman for Cody Meacham. Cody asked her two days ago, apparently unaware she had already committed to another boy."

"The new football jock from Cheyenne?" Capri asked. "Yikes. Hate to say it...but who can blame her?"

Lila reached for a sandwich. "I told her she couldn't do that to Randy. It's tacky."

Capri frowned. "Tacky? Maybe. But I agree, a prom date's not like a dress. You can't just change it without expecting a few...wrinkles."

The room erupted in laughter as they toasted to the complexities of high school dramas and the lessons learned from the crazy ups and downs of growing up.

Reva tucked her legs under her on the sofa, enjoying the warmth of the crackling fire as rain tapped against the windows. A ring at the doorbell pulled her attention. "Who could that be?" she murmured, getting up to answer.

She peeked outside and spotted an Amazon delivery truck parked in the yard. Surprised, she opened the door to find Chet Olson standing on her front deck. "Sorry to bother you, Mayor. I have a delivery. Want me to bring it in?"

"Wow, that was fast." Reva blinked in disbelief. She'd only placed the order the evening before. "Thank you." She motioned him inside, then glanced over her shoulders at the girls and shrugged.

The guy carried in several boxes, making multiple trips in the rain.

Capri got up and came over, her interest piqued. "What's all that?" she asked, inspecting the growing mound of boxes.

"What in the world did you order?" Charlie Grace echoed, joining them.

Reva straightened and lifted her chin. "Nothing. Just a few things for Lucan."

"A few?" Lila's eyebrows arched so high they threatened to merge with her hairline.

Facing her friends' astonished stares, Reva shrugged, adopting a defensive yet light-hearted tone, "Look, I can spoil Lucan if I want to."

Capri laughed. "But we thought by spoiling Lucan you meant buying him a couple of socks and a bib."

Charlie Grace chimed in. "Yeah, I guess we were wrong. You meant the whole internet, apparently!"

20

Lila dug in her purse for her keys as she and Capri pulled into her yard. "Thanks for the ride," she told her friend. "Hey, you want to come in?" They'd wrapped up at Reva's early after noticing their dear friend was nodding off as they visited.

Capri lifted one shoulder. "Sure, why not?"

They exited Capri's pickup, a bright red Dodge D150 Adventurer 'Lil Red Express truck she'd brought home from an auction in Denver, all tricked out with oak wood panels, gold pin-striping over the wheel wells, and dual chrome exhaust stacks. The vehicle was her pride and joy.

Capri followed as they headed for the front porch. "I still can't believe Reva bought all that stuff for Lucan. How many little pairs of cowboy boots does one toddler need?"

Lila laughed. "Apparently, a dozen." She inserted the key into her lock, twisted until she heard a click, then pushed the door open.

There was an immediate shriek as she stepped inside the dimmed living room.

"Mom! What are you doing home?"

Lila clicked on the light. The laughter died on her lips as she stepped into the living room, her eyes widening at the sight before her. "Camille. What in the world?"

On the sofa, amidst a scatter of cushions that looked like they'd been caught in a mild tornado, lay Camille, entwined with the new football jock from her high school. The jock, whose name escaped Lila at that critical juncture, had his arm around her daughter in a way that was a tad too familiar for Lila's comfort. Several buttons were undone on her blouse, adding even more horror to the situation.

Their heads turned towards the door, expressions morphing from surprise to sheer mortification.

Capri, ever the instigator of mischief, couldn't stifle a chuckle, her eyes twinkling with a mix of amusement and nostalgia. "Well, well, what do we have here?" she quipped, her voice laced with a mirth that only served to heighten the tension in the room.

Camille, a flush of embarrassment coloring her cheeks, scrambled to sit up, disentangling herself from her companion with the grace of a newborn giraffe. "Mom! I—I didn't hear you come in. I thought you'd be out longer," she stammered, her voice a mix of defiance and panic.

The jock, now sitting upright but looking as if he wished the earth would swallow him whole, managed a feeble, "Hi, Mrs. Bellamy," before silence engulfed the room, thick and palpable. "I'm Cody Meacham. Uh, we met a while back...at a game," he reminded.

Lila, her initial shock giving way to a measured calmness, set her purse down with deliberate slowness. She fixed her gaze on Camille. "I see we have a guest," she said, her voice steady, betraying none of the turmoil that churned inside her.

Capri, leaning against the doorway with the ease of someone who had navigated many a teenage drama of her own, winked at Camille. "Honey, you've got to pick a better hiding spot. The sofa is the first place any mom checks."

Camille quickly recovered and shot Capri a look that was part grateful, part exasperated. "We were just studying," she ventured, the words sounding feeble, likely even to her own ears.

"Studying," Lila repeated, raising an eyebrow, a smile tugging at the corners of her mouth despite her resolve. She turned to Cody. "It might be time for you to head on home." It was then that she realized she hadn't seen his car out front.

As if knowing what her mom was thinking, Camille quickly explained. "It's parked out back."

The kid jumped up and grabbed the jacket strewn across the back of the sofa. "So, I'll be going, I guess."

The boy, looking for a lifeline, glanced at the open front door.

"Yes, Cody. You should be going," Lila suggested, for a second time. He glanced about, his face filled with impending doom.

Lila nodded, then turned her attention back to Camille. "We'll talk about this later, young lady. In the meantime, I think it's safe to say you won't be going to the prom."

The edict met with immediate protest from Camille, her eyes wide with disbelief and the beginnings of indignation. "But Mom! That's not fair! It was just studying, really!"

Capri, unable to resist, muttered in a playful yet pointed tone, "Ah, the age-old study session that leads to prom cancellation. Been there. Done that."

Lila threw her friend a look before turning back to her daughter. Maintaining her firm stance yet with a hint of compassion, she replied, "Decisions have consequences, Camille. We'll discuss this later, in detail. For now, your focus should be on your actual studies, not...extracurricular activities."

The room fell into a tense silence, the weight of Lila's words settling over them like a thick fog. Camille's shoulders slumped, resignation mingling with her frustration, as she realized the gravity of her mother's decree.

"That's not fair!" She fisted her hands, turned, and stomped toward her room.

Seconds later, they heard a door slam.

"Grounding her from prom is a little harsh, don't you think?" Capri cautiously offered.

Lila rubbed the space between her eyes. "Perhaps. But I don't like him. And I don't like Camille's choices since he came into the picture."

Capri motioned for Lila to follow her into the kitchen, where she pulled out a chair from the kitchen table. "Sit. Are you actually going to make her miss her prom? I mean, she wasn't naked or anything."

"Yeah, we got home in time," Lila said, her voice laced with misery. "Camille used to be so...easy. I don't know what's gotten into her."

Capri chuckled. "I think I know. Did you have a look at that kid? I mean, whew! Every high school girl's dream package."

Lila shook her head with vehemence. "He's the exact opposite of Aaron."

Capri turned sympathetic. "Aaron was one of a kind. They don't make them like your husband."

Lila's eyes flooded with tears. She angrily brushed them aside. "You can say that again. She never even got to know him. If she had, she'd know what to look for in a man."

Capri reached across the table, her hand finding Lila's in a grip that spoke volumes of shared histories and unspoken grief. "Lila, honey. Aaron set the bar sky-high. But you know, he'd want both you and Camille to find happiness, in whatever form it comes. Maybe this Cody Meacham kid isn't the one for your daughter, but she has a good head on her shoulders. She'll find her way."

Lila's gaze drifted past Capri, settling on a framed photograph on the wall, a candid shot of Aaron laughing, his eyes sparkling with life. "I see him in everything we do, Capri. In every decision I make for Camille. I'm just...I'm terrified of letting go, of forgetting even a fragment of him," Lila confessed, her voice barely a whisper. "Even after all these years."

Capri squeezed her hand tighter. "You will never forget, Lila. Aaron's love—it's woven into the very fabric of your being. But it's also okay to make room for new memories, new joys. It doesn't diminish what you had with him. It's not about moving on, but moving forward, with him in your heart."

A silence settled between them, comfortable yet charged with the weight of unshed tears and the warmth of enduring friendship. Lila nodded, a small smile breaking through her sorrow. "Maybe I was too harsh on Camille. Aaron would have found a way to see the humor in it all."

"He would have," Capri agreed, her voice gentle. "And maybe, just maybe, it's time to let a little bit of that humor, that love for life Aaron had, guide you too. Prom night isn't the enemy, Lila. It's just another step in letting Camille grow, and maybe it's a step for you too—a step towards something new."

21

By the following week, Reva realized that as much as she'd wanted to play Wonder Woman, balancing numerous responsibilities amidst constant interruptions and emergencies had become unsustainable. Circumstances had rendered her powerless. She was ready to remove her imaginary indestructible bracelets and lay them down.

Upon reluctantly sharing her ongoing struggles with her girlfriends, the first suggestion they gave was to find a caregiver for Lucan. Accepting this advice did not come easily to her. Each day, she became more captivated by the little boy—his playful antics, his infectious smiles, and his overall cheerful demeanor. The transient nature of fostering weighed heavily on her; she knew it wouldn't last indefinitely. Truth was, she didn't want to miss even a single moment of the gift she'd been given.

Lila quickly reminded her this was how all working mothers felt. "When Aaron was killed, and it was only me...I simply couldn't do it all. I soon realized it was okay to hire some help."

"You should talk to the Knit Wits. I'm sure those ladies

would be thrilled to help you out," offered Charlie Grace. "Once, when Aunt Mo was on a trip and I came down with a stomach bug, those three stepped in and helped watch Jewel. They were a godsend."

Armed with their suggestion, Reva invited Oma Griffith, Betty Dunning, and Dorothy Vaughn over the following day for an informal interview. She pulled a pecan pie, shipped directly from her family's farm store in Georgia, from the freezer and popped it in the oven. She also made fresh whipped cream from scratch. Her friends often teased her about her limited culinary abilities. But she had YouTube, and she knew how to use it.

When the time finally came to transition from a pleasant dessert to the heart of the matter, Reva found herself wracked with a mix of apprehension and determination as she sat down, clipboard in hand.

Nearby, Lucan busied himself with the stack of colorful blocks on a blanket within Reva's constant view. The trio of seasoned, sharp-witted seniors renowned for their knitting prowess and sage wisdom, settled into her plush sofas having finished their pie treat.

Reva fidgeted, trying to maintain a professional demeanor. "Thank you all for coming on such short notice. As you may have heard, I've been struggling to juggle my duties as mayor, attorney, and now mother. It's imperative that Lucan has the best care possible while I don't neglect any of my responsibilities to this town and to my clients." She let out a sigh. "It's a bit much."

Oma Griffith nodded with a gentle smile. "We understand, dear. We've raised a few of our own, haven't we, ladies?"

Betty Dunning chuckled. "Oh, a few might be an understatement, Oma."

Dorothy Vaughn dabbed the corner of her mouth with a

wadded napkin in her blue-veined hand. "Between us, we've probably seen it all. Don't you worry, Reva."

Reva took a deep breath. "Excellent. Now, onto my first question. How are you with crisis management? Say, if Lucan decides to start a small riot or attempts a daring escape?" Her attempt at humor seemed lame, even to her.

Betty laughed. "Darling, we've handled everything from scraped knees to teenage rebellions. A baby-sized riot sounds like a walk in the park."

"And for escapes," Oma said, her eyes filled with mirth. "Betty here used to be quite the sprinter in her day. Weren't you, Betty?"

Betty gave a proud nod. "Still got the medals to prove it."

Reva nodded, slightly reassured, then glanced down at her clipboard. "Right. Next, how familiar are you with the latest in child development theories? I've been reading about the importance of early cognitive stimulation."

Dorothy tilted her head and glanced between her elderly cohorts. "Well, dear, we might not have all the fancy terms down, but we've been stimulating young minds since before it was a theory. Why, just last week, I taught my grandson algebra. He's seven." She leaned to Oma and whispered. "I had to study his textbook all night to pull that one off." She chuckled.

Reva tapped her pen against the clipboard. "How are you with emergency procedures? I have a detailed plan in place in case of any unforeseen events, including, but not limited to, choking, falls, accidental poisoning, burns—"

Before she could finish, Oma waved off her worry. "Betty here is a wizard with a first aid kit, and I've been known to concoct a mean herbal remedy." She turned to the other ladies. "By the way, have you seen that woman on TikTok who warns that if you see a UFO in the sky—"

Dorothy interrupted her well-meaning friend, "And if we find ourselves having to deal with any extraterrestrials, we'll knit them a nice cozy blanket. No one can resist a good pearl stitch, not even aliens."

They all laughed.

Reva finally cracked a smile, her tension easing. "Thank you, ladies. I get your point. I suppose my fears might be a tad…exaggerated."

Oma reached across to pat Reva's hand. "It's all part of being a new mother, dear. We'll take good care of Lucan. And we'll even teach him to knit, won't we, ladies? When he's old enough to hold the needles without hurting himself."

Betty and Dorothy nodded in unison. "Absolutely."

When their meeting concluded and they'd made an agreement to move forward with the shared childcare arrangements, Reva showed the sweet Knit Wit group to the door. She hugged each one tightly and promised to be in touch, thanking them profusely. As she closed the door, she mentally made a list of her instructions, which would no doubt include a compilation of doctor and hospital numbers in case they encountered a medical emergency.

Then she noticed Lucan had helped himself to her purse and had dumped the contents on the floor. Panicked, she beelined over to pick up the items, some of which were dangerously sharp.

As she plucked the keys, receipts, and pens from the floor and nestled them back inside her bag, a tiny business card caught her eye.

Curious, she picked it up.

WARNER AUTO REPAIR—Kellen Warner

REVA SCANNED THE PHONE NUMBER, brows knit together as she tried to recall…oh! The guy who saved her and Lucan from the bear. She'd promised to call him for coffee. Of course, with everything as hectic as it had been, she'd neglected to follow through.

An unbidden, yet rather evocative, image of Kellen on the trail that memorable day vividly materialized in Reva's thoughts. She found herself effortlessly recalling the warmth of his smile, the joyful companionship of his dog by his side, and most notably, the striking physique that he possessed—the way his well-defined build was accentuated by the way his T-shirt clung to his muscular frame, a detail that now lingered prominently in her mind.

She should call him. Especially after he'd helped them on the road that day. Besides, she'd promised.

She fished her phone from where it had fallen between the cushions of her chair and started to dial.

Just as quickly, she clicked it off.

What was she thinking? She had no time as it was. How could she possibly get away for coffee right now?

She sighed and started to put her phone down.

But she'd told him she would call.

The promise nagged at her. She wasn't one to go back on her word.

Taking a deep breath, she overturned her previous decision and called the number on the card. After three unanswered rings, she nearly disconnected, thinking he wasn't there, but then a man's voice answered, "Hello?"

Suddenly, she found herself at a loss for words. "Uh, hi... I'm not sure if you remember me, but my name is Reva Nygard. You once scared away a bear on Highway 26 for me."

"Yes, I remember you," he responded.

Reva's heart raced. She berated herself for feeling as nervous as a teenager, then drew in a deep breath and gathered her composure. "I wanted to express my gratitude for driving away that bear and assisting with my car repairs. Would you be interested in grabbing coffee together?" She waited anxiously for his reply, torn between hoping he would decline and fearing he might accept.

“I’d be delighted,” he answered simply and warmly. “Just let me know the place and time.”

“Fantastic! How about you bring your dog, and I’ll bring my child?” Reva quickly suggested a cozy coffee shop in Jackson known for its exceptional homemade cinnamon rolls. He agreed to meet her there, and after confirming, they ended the call.

Clutching her phone to her heart, Reva walked back to where Lucan was joyfully drumming on the coffee table with his dimpled hands. Watching him, she couldn’t help but beam with happiness buoyed by the little boy’s delight...and hers at the thought of seeing Kellen again.

22

Reva had a relationship with punctuality that bordered on the sacred. She was raised under the stern gaze of her grandfather who taught her as a child that time respects those who respect time. The phrase wasn't just a motto, it was a creed she lived by, embedded deep within her.

Thus, as the sun peeked over the horizon, casting a golden glow over Thunder Mountain, Reva was already up, her day meticulously planned down to the minute. This dedication to punctuality endeared her to the townsfolk and commanded their respect, for they knew, in a world teeming with uncertainties, Reva Nygard's word was as reliable as the sunrise.

Unfortunately, this creed meant nothing to a jammy-faced toddler who ran from her when she came after him with a wet washcloth. When she finally caught up with Lucan and rubbed his dimpled face clean, she glanced forlornly at the highchair tray with the bowl of oatmeal, vowing never to tell anyone she'd bent to his will and replaced the nutritious breakfast—which he refused to eat—with his favorite jam on toast (heavy on the jam.)

By the time she buckled Lucan into his car seat, she was running a solid twenty minutes late for her appointment with Alex, the lead architect on the community center project. She glanced at the clock on her dashboard, mentally calculating the time it would take to get there.

Upon arrival, she discovered Lucan had fallen asleep. She hated to wake him, but leaving him alone in the vehicle was not an option. So, she scooped him up and carried him crying as she made her way to where Alex was standing with a group of men gathered around a makeshift table littered with blueprints.

"Good morning, everyone," she said loudly over the crying child. "I apologize. He just woke up." At that moment, Lucan vomited all over her blouse—a mixture of regurgitated grape jam and peanut butter. "Oh, my goodness!" she exclaimed, holding him at arm's length.

A wide-eyed Alex quickly glanced around at the men. "Do any of you have a—?"

One of the guys, a man with graying hair and deep lines at the corners of his eyes, quickly fished out a clean handkerchief from his back pocket and offered it up. "Don't know why you young guys don't carry one," he said to the other men who stood there stupefied.

Alex took the handkerchief and opened a thermos that was on the table. He wet the cloth with water and handed it off to Reva, who was horrified at the situation. "Thank you," she said, juggling Lucan on her hip, who was now grinning. "My wet wipes are back in the car." She patted the spot on her blouse to no avail. Rubbing it only made the stain worse.

Finally, she sighed. "Looks like a lost cause. I'll have to go home and change." She looked up. "But not this minute. Let's continue." She assumed a professional stance and prepared to participate in the discussion.

The guys all glanced at each other. One of them finally shrugged. "You gonna tell her?" he asked Alex.

"Go ahead," came the reply.

The guy who had posed the question stepped forward and pointed to Reva's head. "Uh, you have a little in your hair."

"What?" Reva's hand darted to where he pointed and met with a sticky concoction. She groaned. How was she going to command a presence with these men and hold their attention with a glob of vomit in her hair?

She met Alex's gaze. "Look, let's reschedule. In the meantime, shoot me an email outlining the progress and any issues that need the city's attention. I'll review it and respond immediately."

She apologized profusely and turned for her car. Lucan leaned over her shoulder and waved his chubby hands back at the crew.

On the way home to change, Reva made a decision. She hit the call button on her steering wheel and activated her voice telephone system. "Call Oma," she said.

Seconds later, the older woman answered. "Well, hello dear."

"Oma, I have a little emergency here." She explained the situation and how she was already running late for her next meeting. She didn't mention the meeting was in Jackson and wasn't business related, but a coffee date with Kellen Warner.

"I'd be happy to watch Lucan, dear."

An hour had passed, and Reva, now showered and in fresh attire, had left the little boy in Oma's capable care. As she accelerated away, a fleeting glimpse in the rearview mirror at the unoccupied car seat stirred an unwelcome sensation of guilt within her. Guilt she quickly brushed aside. After all, Lucan was with Oma—safe, sound, and in the best possible hands.

And she would be fine, too, despite the fact she now had wet hair in a braid. Not wanting to be tardy a second time, she pressed down on the accelerator to make up for the delay, determined to reclaim the lost minutes.

She even let herself enjoy the quiet and reached for the radio dial, tuning into her favorite jazz station. It was a beautiful morning after all, despite its chaotic start.

The piercing sound of a siren broke into her reverie.

A glance in the mirror confirmed her fears as she spotted the red lights of Fleet Southcott's police car. Her gaze darted to her dash and realized her oversight—she'd been speeding.

With a resigned groan, she slowed and prepared to pull over to the side of the road.

So much for her dedication to being punctual.

23

Reva stepped into the Cowboy Coffee Company, the quaint and iconic establishment nestled in the heart of Jackson. The aroma of freshly ground coffee beans mingled with the sweet scent of cinnamon, creating a comforting ambiance. The shop was bustling with the morning rush as tourists lined up to get a cup of their famous arabica bean roast. Despite the demand, the interior had a cozy charm with its rustic wooden tables, soft ambient lighting, and the light murmur of patrons chatting.

She scanned the room and her gaze landed on Kellen Warner, who was seated at a corner table with a clear view of the entrance. He looked up from his coffee, his eyes lighting up as they met hers.

Reva made her way over, her heart skipping a beat. Kellen stood as she approached, showcasing his solid build—every inch the car mechanic who had bravely driven away a bear and expertly changed her flat tire.

"Good morning, Reva," he greeted, his voice warm and inviting.

"Morning, Kellen. I apologize for being late," Reva replied, hoping to atone for her tardy arrival. "I don't normally miss an appointment time," she explained, adding brief details of her complicated morning. "I won't even get into the saga about my flooded office. Apparently, mold can be an issue. The office is going to have to be rebuilt using new materials. The project is expected to take several months. Until construction is complete, I'll be working in some temporary space in City Hall—an area that used to serve as a storage room."

Kellen laughed. "Sounds like quite the day."

She nodded. "It was."

They both sat, and almost immediately, a waitress approached offering to take their order. "You don't want to stand in that line," she offered.

Reva thanked her. She ordered a latte and Kellen asked for another black coffee. They both decided on cinnamon rolls, unable to resist the tantalizing smell wafting from the open display case.

As they waited for their order, Reva found herself admiring Kellen's straightforward demeanor, a stark contrast to the political world she navigated daily. "I admit, I was both surprised and relieved to see you on the road that day. I mean, with the tire and the bear, and all. I was in a bit of a bind," she said, a playful smile dancing on her lips.

Kellen chuckled, a deep, resonant sound. "Well, I guess you could say I have good timing. But honestly, I'm just glad I was there to help. It's not every day you get to play the hero."

Their cinnamon rolls arrived, the sweet, spicy scent of cinnamon making her even more hungry. The rolls were massive, slathered in creamy frosting, still warm from the oven. Reva took a bite, the flavors exploding on her tongue, a perfect blend of sweet and spice.

"This is delicious," she murmured, savoring the taste.

"Yeah, they make the best cinnamon rolls in town," Kellen agreed, taking a bite of his own.

"So, what do you do when you're not saving a damsel in distress?" she asked. "For a living, I mean. Your business card implied you're in an automotive business?"

Kellen laid his fork on his plate. A glimmer of something passed through his eyes as he answered. "I'm a mechanic," he told her. "I fix cars mostly." He shrugged. "That's my occupation, but what I do?" He smiled at her. "I savor life—enjoying all its opportunities. I'm a simple man. Doesn't take a lot to make me content. I'm happy living here in the Tetons, hiking the trails, enjoying the scenery with my dog." He bent and rubbed his golden retriever's ear.

It was the first time Reva noticed he had Max with him.

"What about you?" Kellen asked.

"Me?" She grinned with a shrug. "Well, most of my friends would tell you I'm the opposite. I've been called high maintenance. I love shoes, and purses, and—"

He glanced at her Tory Burch ballet flats. "I noticed."

She grinned a second time. "I like nice things. Always have."

"Yet you are known for your generosity," he remarked.

Reva's brows pulled into a puzzled frown. "How do you know that?"

He offered a casual shrug, a straightforward admission on his lips. "I did a little digging online," he said, without a hint of evasion. "I used your license plate number to find your last name." He lifted his mug slightly to signal the waitress for another round.

"Excuse me?" Reva blinked, taken aback.

He elaborated with ease. "The day we met on the highway, I noted your license plate. I have a gift for details. I figured I'd like to get to know you a bit more—so I looked you up."

His admission dissipated her unease, replacing it with a warmth kindled by the realization he was interested in her.

Her curiosity was now piqued. "So, what did you find?"

"You've built an impressive career as an attorney—

ascending to the role of Thunder Mountain's mayor, a town you've called home since childhood. You were born in Georgia and share ownership of a large pecan farm, which has been in your family for generations." He glanced at her feet again. "Which I suspect funds your proclivity for nice things." There was laughter in his eyes as he said this.

"Wow," she responded. "If you ever want to switch careers, you might lean into being an investigator. You seem to have a knack for sniffing out details that extend far beyond license plate numbers," she teased.

That made him laugh. "That, I do."

As they talked, Reva found herself drawn to Kellen's straightforward honesty and his subtle humor. There was an undeniable attraction between them, a connection that went beyond their chance encounters.

"So, should we make a habit of saving you from wildlife and automotive disasters, or do you think we can find a less dramatic way to spend time together?" Kellen asked, his eyes twinkling with mischief.

Reva laughed, the sound bright and carefree. "I think I'd prefer the less dramatic option. Maybe we can start with something simple, like a hike or another coffee date."

She pulled out her phone and checked her calendar. "How about next week? Is that time good for you?"

Kellen glanced up into the air as if mentally checking his schedule. "Looks like I'm free." When their eyes met, his expression was filled with amusement.

"What?" she asked.

In a surprising move, Kellen reached across the table and took her hand in his. "I'm looking forward to knowing you more, Reva Nygard."

24

"Oh, my goodness! This guy sounds great." Charlie Grace slid a platter of steak nachos across her counter.

"He is," Reva confirmed, reaching for a napkin. "He definitely says what's on his mind. There's no guessing what he's thinking." She picked up the platter and set it on the kitchen table.

"How refreshing. A man who communicates." Lila laughed and pulled a chip from the platter, watching the melted cheese string until it finally broke. "What's his name again?"

Reva opened the jar of salsa. "Kellen Warner. He runs a mechanic shop in Jackson."

Capri stood at the end of the table and gave the martini shaker a few strong jiggles before filling her stemmed glass. "Who all wants one?" Everyone nodded except Reva, who pointed to her diet soda.

"Now, what kind of drink is that again?" Lila asked.

"It's a Mexican Martini. Made with your standard margarita ingredients but spiked with olive juice—à la dirty martini style—and capable of adding a whole lotta olé to this fiesta!"

Capri filled their martini glasses before turning back to Reva. "This Kellen guy doesn't sound like someone you're typically attracted to."

Reva frowned. "What do you mean?"

Capri shrugged and took a sip of her drink, which immediately brought a slow groan. "Dang, that's good. Anyway, it's like this...I date flannels. You date suits."

Reva leveled a look in her direction and reached for a chip. "I beg your pardon?"

Lila quickly nodded in agreement. "Oh, yes. I see what she means."

"You hush and drink your martini. I don't only date suits. And there are a lot of suits that I move on from as quickly as I can." Reva thrust a red-painted fingernail in their direction to emphasize her point. "Do I need to remind you of how badly it went with Bert Reilly?"

Charlie Grace reached for a nacho. "Who?"

"The guy from the dating site you guys set up," Reva reminded. "Without my permission, I might add."

"That doesn't count," Capri told her.

Reva's eyes widened. "Really? Why not? He was an insurance actuary—definitely a suit."

"He's an outlier. There are always some in both categories that you need to leave on read," Capri explained.

Charlie Grace's face filled with exasperation. "Plain language, please."

Lila straightened. "Oh, I know this one. Camille says that means when you read a text but don't respond."

Reva held up both open palms in protest. "I can't believe you guys think I'd only be interested in a professional man." Her mind drifted to Merritt and how badly that relationship had ended, despite her lingering feelings. "I'm open to any guy who has the qualities I admire."

"Which is?" Capri prompted.

Reva took a moment before responding. "Well, I want someone honest, someone who is committed to the relationship, even when things get hard—and there are always difficulties that arise."

Capri laughed. "Call Albie Barton and tell him we have tomorrow's newspaper headline. Reva Nygard is not interested in arm candy. She's looking for a serious relationship."

Reva nudged her friend with her elbow. "You can have the arm candy."

"I'm down for that," Capri replied. She scanned their shocked faces. "What? There's nothing wrong with only wanting to have some fun."

Charlie Grace took the opportunity to speak up. "Well, I suppose arm candy has a place for some people." She grinned in Capri's direction. "But when the right guy appears on the scene—you can't waver. Love doesn't show up all willy-nilly. If this Kellen guy is someone you are interested in, I say go for it."

Reva leaned back in her chair. "Spoken like a woman who has found her man. How is Nick these days?"

Charlie Grace's face softened. "Nick is incredible. Every moment with him fills me with joy, something I hadn't dared dream of finding. And yet, here he is, surpassing every expectation, every hope. I never imagined someone like him could exist." Her smile turned sly, a playful glint in her eye hinting at unspoken secrets before her intense gaze locked onto Reva's. "That's precisely my point. Love has a way of surprising you, of sweeping into your life when you least anticipate it and turning everything upside down. Keep your heart open, Reva. You never know when love might find you."

Reva absorbed her words, allowing the notion to infiltrate the recesses of her mind, contemplating the implications.

Was she open to love again?

The idea was almost too vast to embrace. Her life was a whirlwind of tasks—renovating her flooded office, leading a significant community center initiative, and caring for a young boy who had lost his family, all while managing her usual hectic schedule. People needed her. The thought of embarking on a new relationship was daunting.

BESIDES, new relationships were scary. You had to relinquish control and place trust and faith in someone else. Two things she ran short on.

What did it say that the only true love she'd ever experienced ended with him walking away, choosing his career over her? And the ease with which Merritt moved on, building a life and family with Hillary instead of her, raised questions she dared not voice, even to her closest friends who thought they knew her inside out.

These were the hidden depths of her soul, burdens she bore silently.

"Well, it should make you all happy to know we're seeing each other again this coming week. He texted after we met for coffee and arranged for us to go on a hike with a picnic."

The news prompted a chorus of approval.

"That's wonderful," Charlie Grace said.

Capri pumped her arm in the air. "Yes!"

Lila stood and pulled her into a tight hug. "This makes me so happy."

Reva laughed. "Glad you all approve." She waved her hands. "Now, enough of me and my love life." She turned to Capri. "How's Dick? I didn't see him at the AA meeting last week."

Capri's expression turned sober. "Frankly, the chemo is hitting him pretty hard. He's having a hard time eating, and he's losing weight. Yet the doctor assures us this is all to be expected and that he remains extremely hopeful the treatments will be successful."

"Ah, the cancer journey is never an easy one," Reva replied. "How's your mom?"

Capri sighed. "She watches a lot of QVC. She buys things she doesn't need and puts them on easy pay—then I secretly go into her account and pay off her purchases."

"You're a good daughter," Charlie Grace said before taking a sip of her martini.

Capri turned her attention towards Lila. "And you? Have you come to a decision about Camille and the prom? Is she still banned from attending?"

Lila leaned against the kitchen counter. She crossed her arms and let out a deep sigh. "I caved," she admitted.

This elicited a round of light laughter from the women gathered around the kitchen island.

"Of course, you did," Charlie Grace said, grinning.

"Don't get too carried away with your laughter, Ms. Rivers," Lila cautioned. "Your time will come soon enough."

"Thankfully, that's still a bit down the road for me," Charlie Grace responded, grabbing a napkin. "Right now, Jewel is focused on this new baby coming. She is completely captured by the idea of a little sister."

"Did they find out it's a girl?" Reva asked, curious.

Shaking her head, Charlie Grace clarified, "No, the gender's still a mystery. Lizzy's planning a grand reveal—balloons showering colored confetti. Blue for a boy, pink for a girl."

Capri raised an eyebrow. "How inventive," she remarked dryly. "Though I must admit, those reveal parties flood my TikTok feed. They're quite the rage."

"Well, Lizzy is all about the party aspect of life. God help that little one she has on the way because both my ex and his new wife could use some growing up." Charlie Grace downed her drink. "I'm just saying."

25

Reva slowed her Escalade at the junction of JD Rockefeller Jr. Memorial Parkway and Grassy Lake Road, turning toward where she'd agreed to meet Kellen.

Over the past two days and multiple text messages, they deliberated over the perfect hiking destination. Among the plethora of trails to choose from, they settled on the one leading to Huckleberry Hot Springs—a modest mile-and-a-half trek to a secluded spot only miles south of the border between Grand Teton National Park and Yellowstone where they could enjoy a soak.

The parking area was empty except for Kellen's vintage pickup. Despite a few minor dents adorning the wheel wells, the blue paint gleamed clean and buffed, the chrome meticulously shined.

Kellen casually leaned against the tailgate and watched as she shut off her motor and climbed from the car.

She waved, and he returned the wave, then headed her way.

"You're right on time," he noted, a comment that pleased her.

"Yes, I thought Lucan would fuss a little when I was leaving, but Dorothy distracted him with some hand puppets she crocheted for him. He dumped me and gave his full attention to Mr. Giraffe."

Kellen chuckled. "Kids are fickle."

She retrieved her cap from the front passenger seat and positioned it on her head, letting her long braid hang down the middle of her back. "So, looks like we're not going to run into much of a crowd today," she said, grabbing her backpack and sliding the straps over her shoulders.

"The crowds won't show up until after school is out." He motioned for her to follow him to the trailhead.

The trail to Huckleberry Hot Springs was alive with the vibrant pulse of late spring, the packed dirt path bordered by lush, green meadow grass that swayed gently in the warm yet crisp air. Reva and Kellen moved in comfortable silence, their steps in sync as they navigated the path beneath the vast expanse of blue skies adorned with fluffy, aimless clouds.

"So, Mayor of Thunder Mountain," Kellen began, his tone light and teasing. "Tell me about this job of yours. Are your days spent balancing budgets, or just wild city council members?"

Reva laughed, the sound blending with the soft rustle of the tall pines surrounding them. "Mostly the latter, and I've been known to judge a pie cookoff or two. I've also had the privilege of serving as grand marshal for the annual Zucchini Parade. How about you?"

"A car mechanic's job," he began, playing along with her light-hearted approach, "is a mix between being Indiana Jones and Sherlock Holmes. It turns into quite the adventure, trying to unravel the mysteries of a perpetually clogging oil filter or the curious case of the disappearing brake fluid." His grin widened. "And honestly, I cherish the solitude of what I do. The thought of navigating a sea of conflicting opinions about a TV production some believe is disrupting your peaceful town? That sounds more challenging than any stubborn engine."

"You caught wind of that, did you?" She paused to watch a chipmunk dart across the trail, its tiny brown and white body a flicker of movement before darting into the vibrant green grass.

Kellen nodded, his amusement evident. "Oh, absolutely. The news of that lively debate has traveled far and wide across the county."

The scent of pine mixed with sagebrush filled their nostrils, a natural perfume that invigorated the senses as they continued their hike. The path led them to a rickety wooden bridge, the boards creaking under their weight as they crossed over a babbling creek.

"I'll never get over this beauty," Kellen remarked, gesturing towards the panoramic view offered by their higher vantage point. "Makes you appreciate the little things, doesn't it?"

"It does," Reva agreed, her voice soft, reflective. "Out here, it's easy to forget about council meetings and budget disputes. Nature has a way of putting everything into perspective."

They shared a smile, an unspoken acknowledgment of the serenity surrounding them, the simplicity of the moment, and the promise of their budding friendship.

As they approached the hot springs, the air grew warmer, the sulfur scent of mineral water mingling with the natural aromas of the forest. The sight of the steaming water, nestled like a hidden gem among the trees, was a reward for the hiking journey they had undertaken.

Kellen looked at Reva, a question in his eyes. "Ready for a soak in nature's spa?"

Reva laughed, the sound echoing lightly through the trees. "After navigating the wilds of raising a toddler, this is exactly what I need."

Kellen stripped the backpack from his shoulders and let it rest on a nearby boulder. "How's that going?"

Reva sat on a fallen log and removed her hiking boots. "It's such a gift. I tease about what it's like to chase a rambunctious little boy around all day, but the truth is? I adore him. I savor every moment, knowing the future is unsure." She hesitated, weighing the wisdom of sharing her deepest fear when it came to Lucan. "I know I may have to give him up." She bit the tender flesh inside her mouth before admitting, "I hope to adopt him."

"Wow, that's big," he said with a smile, a genuine expression that reached his eyes. "I find these things have a way of working out the way they're supposed to."

"Yeah, that's what I keep reminding myself," she said, stripping down to her swimsuit.

Kellen offered his hand to steady her as they eased into the edge of the hot springs, dipping their toes into the soothing, warm water.

She could sense Kellen's body right next to her, could feel his arm as it grazed her own.

Kellen looked at her. "Lucan would be lucky to have you."

His words resonated deeply with her as she settled into the steaming water, a warmth spreading through her that wasn't just from the hot springs. "I'd be the lucky one."

They remained submerged in the soothing waters, their eyes drawn to the majestic sight of an eagle gliding gracefully across the sky above. For a few moments, they were silent, lost in the beauty of nature's spectacle. Then, as the eagle disappeared from view behind the tops of pine trees in the distance, they slowly returned their attention to each other.

"Any significant others in your past?" Kellen asked, pulling Reva's attention from its reverie.

Reva, taken aback by the directness, couldn't help but remark, "Wow, you certainly don't beat around the bush, do you?"

He offered a nonchalant shrug, his honesty shining through. "I prefer being straightforward. Dancing around topics—" he paused, locking eyes with her. "It only leads to misunderstandings and wasted time. Life's too short for that. I'd rather we know where we stand, understand each other's journeys and the paths that led us here." He gave her a half-smile. "I'm interested in pursuing a future with you, Reva."

Her eyes lingered on his bare chest for a moment, finding it difficult to breathe.

Reva appreciated his candor and realized the depth of his question was not just being nosy about her past but was his attempt to unlock the potential for what could unfold between the two of them. Nodding, she shared a smile, feeling a newfound respect for Kellen's approach to life.

"In that case," she began, a hint of vulnerability in her voice, "I was in love once. His name was Merritt..."

26

"I was madly in love with Merritt Hardwick—had been since high school," Reva told Kellen.

Kellen's eyebrows lifted. "The political guy who just got busted for financial crimes?"

She nodded. "Yes, that one."

"Wow." He shook his head, the look on his face punctuating his astonishment.

Reva inhaled deeply, her voice now tinged with nostalgia. "Merritt set off for Harvard right after graduation, while I made my way to Tulane. Yet, our connection remained. We talked every day by phone. I never dated anyone else. To my knowledge, neither did he. Our summers were spent reunited in Wyoming, where we were virtually inseparable, only parting when the inevitability of fall sent us back to our respective paths."

Her gaze drifted to the horizon. "Our story took a slight turn when Merritt embarked on his journey to law school. That's when he plunged into the political realm, securing an internship with our state senator. Politics consumed him, his ambitions soaring to the heights of envisioning us as the nation's first couple, nestled in the White House." A faint smile graced her lips at the thought.

"I take it that was not your dream," Kellen prompted.

Reva shook her head. "No. I can't imagine anything worse than residing in our nation's capital city among those who make politics their world."

"But you chose to stay here in Thunder Mountain, eventually stepping into the role of mayor?"

"EXACTLY. Washington, D.C. never called to me. This..." she gestured to the vast landscape enveloping them, "These mountains are where my heart belongs—my home. I could never find fulfillment anywhere else."

They sat in silence for several seconds before Kellen turned to her. "Life is a series of choices."

Reva nodded. "Yes, and Merritt left me."

"Well, the decision was mutual. Right?"

She frowned. "I'm not following."

Kellen gave a slight shrug of his shoulders. "You left him as well. You chose to remain in Wyoming instead of going with him."

The comment ruffled. "I'm not sure that's true. I was madly in love with him," she argued. "And had been for as long as I could remember. We had a deep and lengthy history. It was Merritt who first kissed me. Merritt who snuck in my window at night to study, even though my parents were sticklers about us never being alone in the house without supervision. He was the one who held my hand at my dad's funeral. And it was Merritt who urged me to open my law practice—and later, to step into the role of mayor."

She heard her voice tremble as she added, "I was in a dark place after Merritt left. I numbed my pain with alcohol, a habit

I now have under control, but losing him...well, I lost a part of myself."

"Then why didn't you go with him?" Kellen asked gently.

"Are you suggesting I made a mistake?"

"Not at all. I'm merely highlighting that we all make choices —good, bad, and indifferent. Those choices pave the path to our future. You weren't a victim of the relationship if both of you opted to move on without each other."

Reva's gaze lingered on the blue sky before settling back on Kellen. "You really don't mince words, do you?" She exhaled deeply. "There's truth in what you say. The unfortunate reality is, at times, you're presented with decisions where all options lead to loss."

Kellen looked at her with those dark chocolate eyes as if he could see into her soul. The scrutiny made her uncomfortable.

"Yeah, I'll give you that," he agreed. "It's messy to love after heartbreak. Moving on is painful and it forces you to be honest with yourself about who you are...and what you want."

"Your turn," she challenged, trying to move on. "What's the story behind you being middle-aged and single?"

That made him chuckle. "Ouch! Middle-aged? I'm only in my forties."

"Well, unless you plan on gracing this earth until you're one-hundred and twenty, then, yes, middle-aged."

Their exchange, tinged with humor, momentarily lifted the heaviness of the conversation. Yet, Reva's curiosity had been piqued. She wondered about the experiences that had shaped him, the ones he alluded to with his understanding of love and pain.

He had a story, and she was anxious to hear it.

Kellen was now looking right at her. "I was twenty-six when I married Liz. She was the love of my life."

"What happened?" Reva asked, searching his expression for answers.

In a quiet, somber tone, Kellen began to recount a chapter of his life she suspected he seldom opened. "She was always so vibrant, you know? Even when the doctors diagnosed her with severe coronary heart disease, she faced it with a bravery that made you believe she was invincible."

He paused, seeming to collect his thoughts as if to weave them into a narrative worthy of her memory. "The doctors recommended Coronary Artery Bypass Grafting, CABG. It was supposed to be her way back to a normal life, to alleviate the angina that had been shadowing her every step, to restore the flow of life through her veins."

A wistful smile flickered across his face, but it didn't reach his eyes. "She knew the risks. We both did. But the chance to reclaim a piece of herself, to no longer be defined by the limitations of her condition, was a siren call she couldn't resist."

Kellen's gaze drifted, focusing on a memory only he could see. "The surgery...it was supposed to be routine, but complications arose. An unrelenting infection led to more surgeries and more hospital nights than we cared to count. Each visit, each procedure, I saw less of her. Not just physically, but the spark that made Liz 'her' started to dim."

He let out a long, deep sigh, a testimony to the weight of his words. "In the end, it was her heart that gave out. Not from the disease it bore, but from the battle to fix it. Her decision to move forward with that corrective surgery, it...it cost her everything."

Kellen looked at her then, his eyes saturated with emotion. "That night, I sat on my porch and cried. She was only thirty years old. A day doesn't pass that I don't realize I'm a better man because of how she loved me."

Reva listened, her heart heavy, as Kellen's words painted a vivid, poignant picture of love, hope, and loss. As he concluded, a profound silence enveloped them, the kind that speaks volumes, carrying with it a shared sorrow.

She reached across the small space that separated them, her hand finding his in the water, a gesture of comfort and understanding. Brimming with empathy, her eyes met his. "Kellen," she began, her voice barely above a whisper, laced with the depth of emotion his story had stirred within her. "I... I'm so sorry. For your loss, for the pain you've endured. It's unfair, the way life can unravel, taking with it the dreams and hopes we most hold dear."

Reva's heart ached for him, for the love he had lost and the burden of grief he carried. "Your love for her, it's evident in every word you speak, in the way you honor her memory. Your words are a testament to your wife—beautiful, yet heartbreakingly sad."

She squeezed his hand gently, a silent promise of her presence, her support. "I can't begin to imagine the depth of your pain, but please know, I'm here for you. In this moment, in any moment you need a friend, a listening ear."

Reva's perspective on Kellen started to change. He wasn't just a straightforward kind of guy who was good with his hands; he was thoughtful and complex, with a depth to him that she hadn't noticed before.

Tears, unbidden, welled up in her eyes, not just for Kellen's loss, but for the profound connection they were forging in the shared vulnerability of this conversation. "Thank you for trusting me with her story, with your feelings. It means more than you know."

It dawned on her that Kellen was right. Hiding only robbed you of intimacy. The deepest human connections are forged in these moments of raw openness, where hearts are laid bare. And for the first time in what felt like an eternity, she found herself yearning to connect with a man on a level she never anticipated.

Reva had never revealed the entirety of her soul without hiding—not with Merritt, and not even with her girlfriends.

When she least expected, her world shifted.

Kellen felt something, too. She could tell.

"You know," he said. "You can be lonely even when you're with a lot of people, even when the busyness acts like a shell."

His comment pierced and left her unable to speak.

"I'm lonely, too," he said. "What say we try to shed this isolation together?"

Reva hoped Kellen couldn't see her heart pounding against her chest. Before she could answer, he closed the space between them and kissed her slowly.

Her stomach tightened. She was powerless against the emotions raging inside her. His lips against her own felt wonderful and terrible and scary.

She was heading into unknown territory. If she moved forward, it would be difficult to stop.

She didn't want to.

Without another thought, Reva laid her palm against his face and heard his intake of breath before he deepened the kiss, pulling her closer, and making her head spin. His movements were sure and slow, like everything he did.

For a brief few seconds, she allowed herself to drift away from the demands of those who relied on her, the looming projects on her agenda, and the countless nights spent in solitude.

There were moments in life when it seemed as though the divine playfully stepped in to dazzle and delight. This was undeniably one of those moments. Occasionally, life's joy was so overwhelming that it seemed impossible to hold all the happiness within.

She'd been handed two grand gifts. First, it had been Lucan who arrived on the scene out of nowhere—now Kellen.

She was indeed a woman immensely blessed.

27

The late morning sun spilled golden light through the open windows of Reva's cozy living room, casting warm patterns on the hardwood floor. Today, the world seemed to sing a brighter, more hopeful tune, one that resonated deep within her soul. Reva's heart danced to a rhythm of joy she hadn't felt in ages, buoyed by the unexpected delight of her first date with Kellen.

It wasn't just the laughter they'd shared or the gentle understanding in his eyes when she spoke of her past. Or that he opened himself up and showed surprising vulnerability. It was the realization that the world still held good, kind men—and perhaps, just perhaps, love might find her again.

With this newfound happiness thrumming through her veins, Reva turned the volume up on her Bose stereo. The opening chords of her favorite Fleetwood Mac song filled the room, a timeless melody that captured the lightness of her mood. She extended her hand toward Lucan, who looked up at her with wide, curious eyes. "Dance with me?" she asked, her voice playful.

Lucan hesitated for a moment before a shy smile graced his

features, and he placed his dimpled hand inside hers. Together, they danced around the living room, laughter mingling with the music.

In these moments, with the sun warming her skin and Lucan's laughter echoing in her ears, Reva felt a surge of gratitude. Despite the initial awkwardness and the heavy shadow of loss that had brought them together, Lucan was adjusting, finding comfort in the home that now surrounded him.

Their relationship was blossoming in the most heartwarming ways. Just this morning, Reva had brought Lucan into the kitchen and lifted him onto the counter. He determinedly tried to help make breakfast—a chaotic yet endearing effort that had ended with more eggshells in the omelet than she would have liked. But it was the precious expression on his face, his pure joy and willingness to help, that touched Reva deeply.

They were finding their rhythm, slowly weaving a tapestry of shared experiences. Whether it was their weekend excursions to the community park, where Lucan would excitedly point out every dog that passed by, or their quiet evenings spent reading together before bedtime, each day brought them closer. Lucan's tentative smiles were becoming more frequent, his laughter a regular sound.

Even the childcare arrangement with the Knit Wit ladies was proving to be a blessing. Their willingness to step in and help, offering not just their time but their hearts, had given Reva the support she needed to balance work and home life. Lucan adored them, fascinated by their knitting projects, and often sat beside them with his own little set of toddler-sized needles, clumsily but determinedly trying to mimic their movements.

As the song came to an end, Reva twirled Lucan one last time before pulling him into a warm hug. He wrapped his small arms around her, a gesture of trust and affection that filled her heart to the brim. Looking over his shoulder, out the window to the potted flowers on her sun-dappled deck, Reva felt a sense of true peace settle over her.

A knock at her door pulled her attention. She placed Lucan back on the floor, surprised she hadn't heard anyone pull into the driveway. Of course, she'd been blasting her music loudly.

She opened the door to find Capri standing there. She'd barely pulled the door open when her girlfriend pushed her way in, wearing a wide smile. "So, I hear the date went well?"

Reva cautiously nodded. "And where did you hear that?"

Capri made her way to the kitchen, opened the cupboard, and withdrew a coffee mug. "Dorothy was having breakfast with the rest of the Knit Wits at the Rustic Pine. She said you were glowing when you got home."

"Glowing?"

Capri grabbed the coffee carafe and filled her mug. "Yes, she said you were even humming as you bid her goodnight."

Reva rolled her eyes. "Sounds like Nicola no longer has the corner on the gossip in this town."

Capri waved off the comment and leaned against the counter. Her hair was pinned up inside a cap emblazoned with her company logo—Grand Teton Whitewater Adventures. She wore jeans, a white ribbed tank top that showed off her enviable curves, and a red bandana tied at her neck. "So, spill," she said, taking a sip.

Without waiting for Reva's reply, Capri leaned and ruffled Lucan's hair. "Hey, small guy. How are you today?"

He answered her with a wide grin.

Reva scooped him up and went to work washing off the remaining breakfast from his face. "I like Kellen. He's genuine and smart. But with a sense of humor."

"And not bad to look at," Capri suggested.

Reva let a slow grin form. "And not bad to look at." She felt like a schoolgirl standing here in the kitchen sharing details of a date with her close girlfriend.

She busied herself filling her own coffee cup before turning to her friend. A sly smile nipped at the corners of her lips as she leaned against the counter next to Capri. "He kissed me," she confessed.

Capri spewed out her coffee in shock, then quickly grabbed a napkin and dabbed at her shirt. "What? He kissed you?" She gave her friend an elbow jab. "You slut—giving yourself to a man on the first date."

Reva rolled her eyes a second time. "It was a kiss, Capri."

Capri's hand went to her chest. "What did you do?"

She watched the steam rise from her mug. "I did what any woman would do in the situation—I kissed him back."

It was too much. Capri pivoted and set her mug down. "I can't believe it."

Reva enjoyed her friend's reaction. "I know! I was as surprised as you are. One minute we were talking about past loves—"

Capri stared. "As one does."

"Exactly," Reva said. "And the next, he just leaned in and... kissed me. It was like the world stopped, except for the birds singing.

Capri sighed. "Just like in a Disney movie." She paused. "Did fireworks go off?"

Reva sipped her coffee. "The kiss was truly amazing. No fireworks. Though, I did hear a crow cawing off in the far distance. That counts, right?"

Capri lifted her mug, and they clinked cups. "Of course, it counts."

28

When Reva showed up at Kellen's front door, he was wearing jeans and a white button-down shirt, along with dark brown leather boots like some she'd seen in an L.L. Bean catalog. She leaned in to greet him with a hug and noticed he was also wearing cologne—a smell of cedarwood and clary sage similar to what her dad used to wear on special occasions.

"You look great," he said, motioning her inside.

When she'd dressed earlier, she'd rifled through her closet and finally settled on a pair of black slacks with an off-the-shoulder cashmere sweater and drop earrings to match. A little sexy but not too forward. She had spent additional time applying her makeup. And she, too, had spritzed on a favorite scent—one with the delicate smell of magnolia. Her mother often recited her cherished quote from Coco Chanel: "Wear perfume whenever you wish to be kissed."

On the way out the door, she'd caught a glimpse of herself in the mirror. She looked good. And was glad to hear Kellen thought so, too.

"Thank you for letting me bring Lucan," she said, leading the toddler inside.

Kellen smiled. "I plan to spend a lot of time with you, Reva. Time I know you won't want to neglect spending with this little guy." He beamed down at the toddler who was fascinated with the dog heading their way.

Kellen bent down. "This is Max. Do you want to pet him?"

Lucan looked up at Reva as if to ask if he had permission. She nodded. "His fur is soft. Feel it, baby."

Lucan did as Reva instructed and reached his dimpled hand into Max's gorgeous coat. Delighted, Lucan then plunged his wide-eyed face against the dog's coat and let out a happy giggle. "Dog. Dog," he said.

Max emitted a joyful bark and wagged his tail.

Kellen's face broke into a wide grin. "Looks like those two are going to get along just fine."

He led them into the kitchen and motioned for her to take a seat at the counter where he put a drink in front of her. "That's cucumber mint lemonade," he said, pouring himself a glass.

Reva took a sip. "Oh, wow. That's really good."

Her compliment seemed to please him. "I hope you like beef stroganoff. It's one of my signature dishes."

She lifted her nose into the air. "Smells delicious."

"Yeah, and I figured the kid would like the noodles better than my beef Wellington."

Reva looked at him over the top of her glass. "So, you cook?"

He nodded. "I do. And from what I hear, like me, you love good food."

"Where did you hear that?"

He laughed a little. "I ran into Bear Country Gifts the other day when I was in Thunder Mountain. I wanted to pick up a little something to send to my sister for her birthday. The owner—Dorothy Vaughn—started up a conversation about you. She says she watches the little one on occasion."

Reva groaned inside. "Yeah? What else did she tell you?" Dorothy seemed to have taken far too much interest in her budding love life.

"Nothing, except to tell me how loved you are and that no one in Thunder Mountain wants you to be hurt. Seems your constituents are a protective bunch."

"That they are," Reva admitted. "So, be warned. They are all watching. My most avid guardians are my girlfriends."

This brought a slight smile to his face. "Noted."

She turned to check on Lucan. "Oh, my goodness! Is that a cello?" She pointed to the instrument in the corner of the living room.

Kellen nodded. "Yup."

"You play the cello?"

"You sound surprised," he said, turning for the stove. He lifted the lid on the simmering pot and stirred the stroganoff.

Her surprise was evident, a stark contrast to the initial impression she had formed of Kellen, a mechanic with grease-stained hands and a straightforward demeanor. In her mind, the worlds of auto repair and classical music seldom intertwined. Yet here was Kellen, embodying a bridge between these disparate realms with a casual ease that intrigued her.

"I guess I am," Reva admitted, her gaze shifting from the cello back to Kellen. "It's just that...you don't meet many mechanics who play the cello."

Kellen chuckled, a sound that seemed to carry a hint of pride. "Well, my mom was a music teacher. She believed that music was essential for expressing emotions and understanding the world. So, she made sure I learned."

The cello poised next to a table stacked with Popular Mechanics magazines cast a new light on this man—a revelation that made Reva recognize there were often very unexpected facets of people.

As Kellen returned to his culinary task, Reva found herself

drawn to the idea that Kellen was multifaceted—and was capable of nurturing both the practical and the artistic aspects of life.

After they'd finished the main course and enjoyed a dish of ice cream smothered in fresh strawberry puree, Reva urged him to play for her. "I'd love to listen."

Kellen wiped his hands on the dish towel. With a modest smile, he said, "Sure, what do you want to hear?"

She carried Lucan into the living room and sat on the sofa, kissing the top of the sleepy little boy's head as he nodded off. "You choose."

Moving gracefully to the instrument, he lifted it with a familiarity and affection that only years of practice could bring. The room filled with an anticipatory silence as he positioned the cello between his knees, the bow poised above its strings.

Choosing a piece that seemed to hold a special place in his heart, Kellen began to play "The Swan" from Saint-Saëns' *Carnival of the Animals*. The notes flowed with a gentle, melancholic beauty, filling the space with an ethereal quality that seemed to suspend time. The melody, both elegant and deeply emotional, spoke of longing and serenity, of delicate strength.

Reva watched, utterly captivated. The music swept over her, weaving a spell of tranquility and wonder. It was as if the cello's voice, under Kellen's expert guidance, was narrating a story too profound for words. She found herself moved by the performance, her earlier intrigue blossoming into a deep appreciation for the man before her. His ability to express such vulnerability and grace through music revealed layers of sensitivity she hadn't anticipated.

How could one man masterfully navigate both the gritty world of socket wrenches and the emotional depths of a musical composition, playing with such beauty and heartfelt expression?

. . .

As the last note lingered in the air, a heavy, satisfying silence fell. Reva, her eyes shining with emotion, broke the quiet. "That was beautiful, Kellen," she said, her voice soft but sincere. "I've never heard anything quite like it."

Kellen's eyes found their way to hers. The room seemed to hold its breath as he laid the bow aside and moved to her. He gently lifted the sleeping toddler from her arms and nestled him onto the sofa cushions, then pulled a blanket over him. Then he held out his hand to Reva.

She stood, and he pulled her into an embrace, his face nestled against her hair.

Reva pulled back and looked up at him, her heart thrumming in her chest. Kellen paused, just a breath away, his gaze searching hers for permission, for a sign. In the quiet, Reva's soft, affirmative whisper barely broke the silence. "Kellen."

As she said his name, he gently reached out, his hand brushing a stray lock of hair behind her ear, his touch sparking a trail of warmth down her spine. Reva's eyes fluttered closed, anticipation tingling at the very tips of her fingers, her breath hitching as she sensed him drawing nearer.

Kellen's lips met hers, a soft, hesitant contact that spoke volumes, a question and an answer all at once. The world seemed to stand still. The only reality was the sensation of his lips against hers, tender yet full of emotion. Reva responded in kind, her hands finding their way to his shoulders, pulling him closer, deepening the kiss. It was a kiss that unfolded slowly, exploring, and affirming, a gentle claiming of mutual desire and recognition of the connection that had sparked between them.

As they finally parted, breathless and with hearts racing, their eyes met again, holding onto the moment, the unsaid words hanging between them like stars in the night sky. For those few, precious seconds, everything else faded into the background, leaving only the profound realization of a bond that had been irrevocably formed.

Just then, Reva's phone shattered the silence, its ringtone slicing through the air. She blinked, pulled abruptly from the spell, and fumbled for her phone. Glancing at the caller ID, she saw it was Lila. With a reluctant sigh, she answered, her heart still racing from the moment before.

"Lila, what's up?" Reva asked, trying to steady her voice.

"Lizzy's gone into labor, and it's chaos over here! Gibbs is MIA, and Charlie Grace just left in a hurry after Jewel called her, panicking. We need you, Reva," Lila's voice was a mixture of excitement and stress. "Charlie Grace is fit to be tied."

The news snapped Reva back to reality, the romantic bubble bursting as duty and concern took over. She met Kellen's eyes, seeing understanding and a touch of disappointment mirrored there.

"I have to go." Her voice carried a mix of apology and urgency as she quickly explained the situation. When one of them needed the others, they all dropped everything and came.

Kellen nodded, the warmth in his gaze undiminished. "Of course. Go. I'll be here if you need anything. In fact, I can keep and watch Lucan if it helps."

Reva hesitated. She wasn't ready to end their time together —not after that kiss. "Would you come with me?"

"Sure, if you want me to," he told her.

With a grateful smile and a promise to make all this up to him, Reva gathered the sleeping little boy, wrapping him tight with a blanket, and hurried for the door. Kellen grabbed his keys from the hook and followed.

Soon after, they pulled into the parking lot in front of Thunder Mountain Medical Clinic, a two-story house with a wraparound porch that had been converted to serve their community for routine medical needs. The second floor included a six-bed senior living center.

The establishment was run by Dr. Eldred Dickerson and his nurse assistant, Wanda. Dr. Ed, as he was called, was now in his late sixties. Wanda was no spring chicken. Both were known for their warmth and unyielding dedication to their patients, often going above and beyond the call of duty to ensure everyone received the care they needed. The clinic, with its homey facade, had become a beacon of comfort and healing in the community.

As Kellen and Reva stepped out of the car, the evening air mingled with the scent of fresh flowers that lined the pathway to the entrance. The welcoming sound of the clinic's old-fashioned doorbell rang through as they opened the front door, a sound that had greeted countless visitors over the years. Inside, the walls were adorned with photographs of the community and framed thank-you notes from patients, telling stories of healing and hope. The reception area, cozy and inviting, was manned by Sarah, the receptionist, who greeted them with a warm smile. Dr. Ed's reputation for treating patients like family was not just commonly known; it was felt by all who entered the Thunder Mountain Medical Clinic.

The reception area buzzed with energy tonight, the small waiting room now overflowing. As Reva stepped in, Lila and Capri quickly approached her with an update. "Lizzy's already at the pushing stage," Lila told her, eyes wide with excitement.

Reva's gaze swept the room, searching. "Where's Charlie Grace?" she asked, concern threading her voice.

From a corner seat, Jewel popped up, her voice bright, "Mom's in the back, helping out with everything."

Capri leaned closer, her voice dropping to a conspiratorial whisper. "Charlie Grace, you know, always picking up after Gibbs' messes."

Reva's eyebrows arched in surprise. "He's not here?"

"No," confirmed Lila with a nod, her expression a mix of disappointment and resignation.

Aunt Mo made her way over, her presence commanding yet warm. She placed a comforting hand on Jewel's shoulder, smiling down at her. "Looks like you're going to be a big sister very soon, aren't you, Puddin'?" Her eyes twinkled with wisdom as she glanced at the group, her manner too gracious to openly criticize Gibbs in front of his daughter.

She then extended a hand to Kellen, her voice filled with warmth. "And you must be the gentleman I've been hearing about—Reva's new friend."

As Reva introduced Kellen, her attention drifted to Albie. Lizzie's uncle stood awkwardly by the coffee table, his hands clenched around a Styrofoam cup, his anxious gaze darting towards the hallway as if expecting someone or something to emerge at any moment.

At that moment, the entrance door burst open, and Gibbs made his entrance, disheveled and breathless. He ran a hand through his unkempt hair, urgency in his voice, "Where is she?"

Albie's reaction was immediate and visceral. His Styrofoam cup hit the table with such force that coffee erupted over the checkerboard pattern of the tablecloth, red and white now marred by dark stains. "Where have you been?" he demanded, his tone loaded with accusation.

Gibbs, visibly uncomfortable, attempted to deflect with an evasive, "With a...friend," his voice trailing off under the weight of the collective disapproving groans filling the room.

Capri leaned to Reva and whispered, "Does anything work above that boy's neck?"

Reva gritted her teeth. "I think we know which of his body parts work best."

Albie's temper flared, and he advanced towards Gibbs, hands clenched as if ready to choke him.

Reva acted swiftly, her grip firm on Albie's wrist. "Albie, that won't solve anything," she warned. She took a moment, choosing her words with care. "This...situation can be addressed later. For now, our priority is Lizzy and the baby."

For added measure, her head tilted in the direction of Jewel, who watched the unfolding event with wide eyes.

Her intervention snapped Albie back to reality. He relaxed, albeit slightly, his nod reluctant yet acknowledging the sense in her words. His glare lingered on Gibbs, who managed a sheepish look of gratitude towards Reva.

Reva's response was sharp, her disdain clear. "I didn't do it for you," she said, her voice low yet laced with contempt.

She turned to face Kellen and her sleeping child. "Thunder Mountain is never short on drama," she whispered.

He grinned back at her, looking impressed as he whispered back. "You're a force to be reckoned with, Ms. Nygard."

Lila pushed Gibbs toward the hallway. "Go! Go!"

Gibbs did as he was directed.

Minutes later, the entry door opened again, sending the little bell ringing. This time, Nicola Cavendish and her husband, Wooster, entered the room. Trailing them was Fleet Southcott, the town deputy.

Nicola quickly surveyed the gathering. "No baby yet?"

They collectively confirmed the baby had not yet arrived.

Fleet held out a box of cigars. "For when the time comes," he said, with a hint of a smile. "I figured we'd all want to celebrate properly."

Albie, who had now begun pacing near the fireplace, took the box with a nod. "Thank you, Fleet. That's thoughtful of you."

Nicola parked her hands on her hips. "So, how's the little mama doing?" she asked, her gaze fixed on the door leading to the hallway and the room where the event of the hour was unfolding.

"Lizzy started pushing a while ago," came Capri's reply. "Shouldn't be much longer now."

Wooster leaned against the reception desk, watching the small group gathered in anticipation. "This town hasn't seen a birth in a while. It's good news, really good news."

Albie finally stopped pacing. His face finally broke into a smile. "It is. After everything that's happened this year, we needed some good news."

The conversation lulled as each person retreated into their thoughts, the air filled with the shared understanding of the hope this new life represented. Outside, the wind whispered through the trees, as if nature itself was joining in the wait for the new arrival.

The door leading to the hallway creaked open, and Gibbs appeared, a broad smile stretching across his face, lighting up the room with a joy that was almost tangible. Behind him, Charlie Grace stepped in, her expression a mirror of Gibbs', though tinged with a bit of exhaustion.

"It's a boy," Gibbs announced, his voice rich with emotion. "Both mother and child are doing splendidly."

A collective sigh of relief and happiness swept through the room, followed by a chorus of congratulations and the sound of clapping hands. The atmosphere was electric with joy, a stark contrast to the tense anticipation that had filled the space just moments before.

Jewel, who had been perched on the edge of her seat, her small hands fidgeting with the hem of her dress, looked up at her mother with wide, expectant eyes. "Can I see the baby now?"

Charlie Grace knelt beside her daughter, her eyes softening. "Yes, sweetheart. Let's go meet your new brother." She extended her hand, which Jewel took eagerly, and together, they made their way toward the hallway. Gibbs grinned widely before turning to follow them.

After taking several steps, he paused and turned to Albie. "You coming?"

Albie beamed. "You bet!"

The group parted to let him through, their faces alight with warm smiles and nods of encouragement. As Charlie Grace and Jewel moved down the hallway, the murmur of conversation resumed behind them, now filled with stories of births and babies, a fitting soundtrack to the new beginning unfolding down the hall.

Reaching the closed door, Charlie Grace gently grabbed the doorknob and pushed it open to the room where Lizzy lay, a tiny bundle cradled in her arms. Jewel tiptoed closer, her curiosity mingling with a hint of awe at the sight of her new sibling.

"Say hello to your brother, Jewel," Charlie Grace whispered, her voice filled with emotion as she guided her daughter closer.

Jewel leaned over, peering at the sleeping infant with fascination. "Hi, baby brother," she whispered, a gentle smile blooming on her face. The little girl glanced at Lizzy. "What's his name?"

"Bodie Albie Nichols," Lizzy announced, looking worn yet happy.

"After my grandpa...and Lizzy's favorite uncle," Gibbs added, with his hand on Jewel's back.

"A fine name," Albie said, tears welling. He gave Gibbs' back a hearty slap. "A right fine name."

In that quiet room, under the soft glow of the moonlight filtering through the curtains, a new chapter began—and a sweet new addition was welcomed into the residents of Thunder Mountain.

29

The warm glow of the setting sun bathed Lila's modest living room in a cozy light, casting long shadows across the mismatched furniture that hinted at garage sales and hand-me-downs. The walls, adorned with military photos and children's artwork, vibrated with the excited chatter of Reva, Lila, Capri, and Charlie Grace, who were gathered for their regular Friday night get-together. Tonight, however, was far from ordinary; they were helping Lila's daughter, Camille, get ready for her prom.

"Can you believe Camille is going to prom already?" Lila exclaimed, adjusting the creased sofa cushions, her voice a mixture of pride and disbelief. The house, though small and worn, was meticulously clean with everything in its place.

Lila handed a stuffed teddy bear to Lucan, who beamed as he lifted it from her hands and brought it to his face, kissing it.

"I swear, it feels like yesterday we were fussing with our own dresses, trying not to trip on our heels," Reva replied, laughing as she helped lay out Camille's accessories on the coffee table, which bore the marks of many a family game night.

"Well, that's a skill you've definitely mastered as an adult," remarked Capri. "Even Cinderella would be jealous of those little Prada numbers I saw on your feet the other day."

Capri motioned to her worn hiking boots. "A real woman isn't afraid to wear L.L. Bean," she teased.

Lila sighed. "I nearly choked when I saw the price of Camille's shoes. Half a paycheck for those little numbers. I decided to splurge for her prom. She'll remember this night forever." She sighed again. "I certainly remember ours."

Charlie Grace, the photographer of the group, was in charge of the camera equipment, checking the settings to ensure the photos would capture the night perfectly. "Remember how we all crammed into my dad's old station wagon? We were so squished with our dresses and hairdos, afraid to ruin them before we even arrived!" she reminisced, prompting laughter from everyone.

Capri, who had always had a flair for fashion, was carefully applying the finishing touches to Camille's makeup. "You're so lucky, Camille. We didn't have YouTube tutorials back then. I had to guess my way through eyeliner and ended up looking like a raccoon!"

Camille, sitting patiently, her eyes sparkling with excitement and a hint of nervousness, could barely keep still. "I can't wait to show you guys those shoes Mom bought me to go with the dress Aunt Mo made. Mom, do you think they'll like them?" she asked, turning towards Lila with a hopeful look.

Lila smiled warmly, her heart swelling with love for her daughter. "They'll adore the gown and shoes just as much as I do. You will look beautiful, sweetheart."

As Camille disappeared to put on her dress, the women found themselves drifting into their own memories of prom night, each sharing stories of teenage dreams and minor disasters.

"Remember the year we concocted that oatmeal scrub from

the recipe in your mom's *Harper's Bazaar* magazine?" Reva asked Capri, as she lifted Lucan and positioned him on her hip. "And gave ourselves a pre-prom facial?"

"The one that nearly scrubbed the skin off our faces? We barely had enough CoverGirl to cover our red skin."

"Andy Denman didn't mind," Charlie Grace teased. "Seems to me he wouldn't have cared if your skin was teal green."

Capri sighed. "Yeah, dancing with him in the gymnasium decorated with twisted strips of colored crepe paper...that was the best." She paused. "Or maybe it was the after-party out at the end of Dog Alley with the case of bottled Zima."

Reva laughed. "Dog Alley. I forgot we used to call it that."

"Because of old Earl Bennett's yapping border collies," Charlie Grace offered. "Those dogs would carry on barking every time you drove past his place."

When Camille reentered the room, the conversation halted abruptly. She stood there, transformed, in a floor-length dress that seemed to capture the very essence of spring—a dress made of hot pink satin with silver princess-heel shoes. Her friends and her mother were momentarily speechless, caught in the magic of the moment.

Capri finally broke the silence, her voice thick with emotion. "Oh, Camille. You look absolutely stunning."

The room filled with exclamations of agreement and admiration as they all gathered around Camille, adjusting a strand of hair here, smoothing the fabric of the dress there, each action a symbol of their collective support and love.

"You look beautiful," Reva said. "You're going to be the prettiest girl there."

The doorbell rang and Lila answered, pulling the wooden door open. Randy Eisman stood there in a tux, holding a clear plastic container with a beautiful corsage inside.

Reva leaned to Capri. "Randy Eisman? I thought she dumped him for Cody Meacham?"

Capri chuckled. "Keep up—that was last week."

"Alright, everyone, let's take those pictures. We can't let this moment slip by," Charlie Grace announced, herding the couple into position with an expert eye for detail. She followed with shots of Lila and her daughter, another with Lila and the prom couple, and finally with a group photograph of them all.

As the flash of the camera captured each scene, the images preserved were more than just snapshots of Camille's prom preparation. The photos served as evidence of the bonds of friendship, the passage of time, and the shared joy of life's milestones.

Before they knew it, it was time for Camille and her date to head out. As everyone bid them goodbye, Lila gave a final hug. She closed the door, turned, and broke into tears.

Reva rushed to her side. "Oh, honey! What's the matter?"

"Nothing," Lila sobbed, brushing tears from her cheeks. "It's just...well, I'm having one of those moments. So good it's almost sad because I'll never be this happy again." A fresh stream of tears bloomed. "And Aaron is missing it. He'll miss all these milestones—prom, wedding, first grandchild."

The three women all surrounded her with tight hugs and offers of encouragement.

"He'd be so very proud of Camille," Charlie Grace said.

Reva squeezed Lila a little tighter. "You've done a marvelous job with her, Lila. And all on your own."

Lila sniffed and glanced among her girlfriends. "Well, not entirely on my own. You've all been in my corner. I love you girls so much."

"Same," stated Reva. "You've all been there for me time and time again. When Merritt crushed me by leaving, and most recently with me deciding to foster little Lucan."

Charlie Grace nodded. "Do I need to remind you who built my website for Teton Trails? Do you think I would ever have been brave enough to step out into that new venture without the support of you three?"

Capri added her own comment. "How about all those nights I spent at your houses back when I was a kid and Dick was drinking and out of control?"

The four women stood in that embrace for several seconds, for in the end it was the love and support they found in each other, the understanding and acceptance, that were their greatest strengths, their most precious treasures.

"We're friends, real friends," Reva stated. "And that means, no matter what life brings, we'll still be here."

30

Morning rumbled in with a distant clap of thunder and put an end to Reva's sleepless night. She rose from her bed, groggy and feeling exhausted, and opened the window slightly. A brisk, northerly wind carried the scent of rain through the tops of the pines. She basked in the aroma long enough to clear her head, then slowly pushed the window frame closed before the chill filled the room.

Lucan was coming down with a cold. He'd coughed most of the prior night and his nose was stuffy, which prompted her to get up in the middle of the night to scan the internet for potential remedies. With so many conflicting choices, she'd finally given up and called Charlie Grace who promptly told her to rub the tiniest bit of vapor rub and place a warm wet washcloth on his chest. The treatment provided instant relief and Lucan fell into a deep sleep.

Even then, Reva could barely bring herself to place him back in his toddler crib. Instead, she carried him to her own bed and cradled him against her body, laying her head on top of his soft curls until she, too, dozed off.

From the moment she'd held Lucan for the first time, a flood of emotions overwhelmed her—joy, fear, and a profound sense of responsibility. No amount of reading or advice could have prepared Reva for the reality of motherhood. Every cry was a mystery, every smile a triumph.

She doubted every decision, from how tightly to fasten his car seat to deciphering the hunger cries from the tired ones. The nights blurred into days, and the exhaustion was unlike anything she'd ever experienced. Especially when she had to juggle motherhood with so many responsibilities.

Yet, with each passing day, she learned. Reva grew alongside Lucan, discovering strengths she never knew she possessed and a love so deep it anchored her through the storm of uncertainty. Motherhood, with all its challenges and without prior experience, had been her greatest teacher, showing the depths of her resilience and the boundless capacity of her heart.

In a nutshell...she adored this little boy beyond anything she could ever have imagined.

So, when her phone dinged on her way downstairs, she never could have contemplated the terror a three-lined message from his social worker could bring—even when she knew deep down this day might come.

"Reva, we'd had an unexpected development with Lucan. You need to bring him to the office this morning along with his things. I'll explain when you get here."

Her heart pounded against her chest wall as her mind raced through possibilities and what the message could mean. "...and bring his things." That couldn't be good.

Her mind went into autopilot as she took a deep breath. First things first. She'd need a shower, and she'd have to feed and dress Lucan. Then they'd make the trip to Jackson and find out what all this was about.

She fought valiantly to maintain her composure, yet her

hands trembled as she selected a pair of tiny jeans and a long-sleeve shirt adorned with a puppy, his cherished outfit. The puppy emblem, soft to the touch, featured a tail designed for gentle strokes.

With a resolve to stay strong and not preemptively worry, she made her way to the shower. As hot water cascaded down her back, she lathered her hair, pondering whether any family had been discovered, apart from a grandfather behind bars.

Inwardly, she harbored a selfish hope that no other relatives would come forward.

For a fleeting moment, as she later secured Lucan in his car seat and arranged his bags in the back, the thought of reaching out to her friends crossed her mind. The prospect of facing potentially devastating news without Charlie Grace, Lila, and Capri seemed daunting.

However, after a moment of reflection, she decided not to. They would undoubtedly rally to her side, but without knowing the specifics of the situation, it was premature to disrupt their lives.

Instead, she chose to confront whatever awaited her solo. She would attend the meeting with the social worker and face whatever challenges lay ahead, armed with the knowledge that she could call on her friends if the need arose.

Despite her resolve, Reva's mind wandered into crazy places on the drive to Jackson.

The prospect of saying goodbye to Lucan was not just about parting with the child she had grown to love; it was also about confronting the realization that she wanted to be his legal mother. This unexpected chapter in her life had shown her a future she now yearned for—a future that included Lucan, and possibly more children, laughter, and the chaos of family life.

As Reva considered potentially handing Lucan over to someone else's care, she couldn't help but feel a sense of loss for the life she was only just beginning to imagine for herself. The journey with Lucan had been a gift, offering her a glimpse into a part of herself she was now unwilling to ignore. Regardless of what the future held, this experience had irrevocably changed her, highlighting a desire for motherhood that would shape her decisions moving forward.

She desperately wanted to remain Lucan's mother...forever.

Reva stepped into the starkly lit lobby of the Family and Child Services building, her boots echoing on the polished floor as she crossed to the reception desk. "I'm Reva Nygard. I'm here to see Bea Followill."

The clerk nodded. "Yes, Ms. Followill is expecting you."

As Reva stood, clutching Lucan a little closer, she saw Bea Followill approaching through the lobby.

"Reva, thank you for coming on such short notice," she said, her face no longer filled with calm demeanor and a compassionate smile, but concern. A concern that only heightened Reva's apprehension.

Dressed in a fitted pantsuit in a shade of gray that matched the stormy sky, Bea exuded an air of professional demeanor. As she drew nearer, her expression conveyed a mixture of understanding and sadness, a silent acknowledgment of what the horizon held.

"Like I said in my text message," Bea began, leading them to her tiny office. "We've had an unexpected development."

Reva trembled inside as she took a seat and unwrapped Lucan from his jacket. "What news?" Her voice remained steady despite the turmoil she felt inside.

Bea folded into her office chair and let out a sigh—a long, heavy sound that seemed to carry more weight than the air could hold. "His grandfather has reached out to us through legal counsel. Despite currently serving time in Texas for armed robbery—" She paused, searching Reva's eyes. "Jess Dorsey wants to start proceedings for full custody."

"I—I'm not following."

"Technically, Lucan's grandfather is his legal guardian until he relinquishes or the courts rule otherwise. Either way, he has about eight months left to serve out his sentence. Based on the circumstances surrounding this situation, his attorney is petitioning the court for early release, hoping to convince the judge it's in Lucan's best interest for his grandfather to be freed so his grandson can live with him."

Reva scowled with concern. "He's a criminal," she protested. "I mean, is he the best one to care for Lucan? I am more than willing and able to—"

"I'm afraid there's little we can do if Mr. Dorsey wants to pursue custody. Of course, we'll be completing a family home study but the fact he has a charge of this nature in his background doesn't necessarily preclude him from stepping in as Lucan's only family and taking custody of his grandson." Bea looked across the desk patiently. "Given the current situation, we have no choice but to accommodate the rules and procedures in place. Lucan is currently a ward of the state, and we take that responsibility seriously."

Bea folded her hands on her desk. "Reva, you know we'll do everything we possibly can to ensure Lucan Dorsey is safe and in the best possible place he can be. Sometimes my personal desires do not line up with how the court rules. Please understand we do all we can," Bea implored, her eyes pleading.

The room seemed to spin as Reva processed Bea's words. She thought of the hours she'd spent holding Lucan through the night, comforting him, and the surprising amount of love she already felt for this little guy in her lap.

The possibility of handing Lucan over to a distant, incarcerated relative whose only goal was to walk away from prison was unthinkable.

"Bea, Lucan is...happy. He's well cared for." Reva tried to articulate the storm of objections in her mind, but each quickly dissipated, sounding less convincing than the last. She nearly screamed the *only* thing that mattered here. "He's been through enough already. What is he going to think if the courts take him from me? He's going to feel like I abandoned him." She let out a rare curse. "We can't do that to him." She refrained from adding the other important thought in her mind. "He's mine!"

"I understand your situation, Reva. You've been doing an amazing job. No one could have done better," Bea said, her sincerity unmistakable.

The silence that followed was filled with unspoken fears. Reva felt a knife at her heart, ready to plunge its sharp edge into everything she held dear. She couldn't imagine abandoning Lucan to anyone else—and especially a convict. Even if he was Lucan's grandfather.

She let her lips drop to the top of his soft, black curls and kissed him. He turned and looked up at her, his large, brown eyes filled with nothing but trust.

"Okay, what now?" Reva finally managed, her voice a mixture of trepidation and worry. "You asked me to bring his things. Lucan has already become a part of my life. Does that mean I can't take him home with me?" She could barely push the words past the lump in her throat.

Bea's sadness was palpable. "I'm afraid that is best, Reva. I can't tell you how much harder this will be later—on both of you."

The following hour was a blur. Paperwork signed, instructions given, court dates noted. And tears shed...lots of tears.

Especially when she kissed his soft, dimpled cheek and whispered, "I love you, Lucan."

As Reva pushed through the doors of the Family and Child Services building and made her way to the car without Lucan in her arms, more tears blinded her path.

There had been losses in her life—yet nothing like this. Yes, she'd always known this was a possibility, but never truly believed she'd have to give him up. Leaving Lucan in Bea Followill's arms and walking away without him felt like death. Worse than death.

Abandoning Lucan to some unknown fate was torture.

31

Reva sat at her table, her eyes red and swollen from crying, a tissue crumpled in her hand. Her girlfriends—Charlie Grace, Lila, and Capri—hovered around her with concern, the mood somber, the air heavy with empathy and unwavering support.

Charlie Grace reached and covered Reva's hand with her own. "Reva, honey, you did what you had to do. Lucan...he'll be well taken care of until all this gets sorted out."

Reva shook her head, a fresh wave of tears spilling over. "But it feels like I've abandoned him. Like I've torn away a piece of my own heart and left it behind. How does someone do that? How?" She moaned, her heart nearly breaking.

Lila patted her friend's back gently. "Because you love him. Sometimes, love means making the hardest choices for their sake, not ours."

Capri parked her hands on the hips of her tight jeans. "Baloney. I'm with Reva. How could this possibly be in Lucan's best interest? He should be with her. She stepped up, opened her heart and home, and now they do this to her?" She shook her head angrily. "Makes no sense whatsoever!"

Reva looked up at them through tear-filled eyes. "What if he thinks I don't want him? What if he believes I gave him away because I don't care? He's so little. First his mom and dad, and now me?" She buried her head in her hands. "It's cruel on all levels."

As an attorney, Reva was acutely aware of the extensive influence wielded by the court, recognizing its capacity to effect both beneficial and detrimental outcomes. She understood that, similar to any government entity, the court operated within a framework of boundaries, regulations, and bureaucratic requirements that did not always align with the principles of justice.

Charlie Grace glanced between the others with conviction. "We'll help you stay in touch, visit, whatever it takes. Lucan will know how much you love him."

Lila nodded her approval. "Yeah, and we're here for you, too. You're not going through this alone, Reva. Not for a single second."

Capri slid a cup of tea toward Reva, a small but meaningful gesture of comfort. "You're the bravest person I know, Reva. Facing this, doing what's best for Lucan despite the pain it causes you...that's true courage."

Reva sniffed and reached for a fresh tissue. "I just miss him so much already. It's like...it's like I've lost a limb."

Lila stood and clapped her hands, signaling she had an idea. "Let's plan something, okay? Something for Lucan. Maybe start putting together a little care package or a photo album of you two. Something he can look at in the years to come and remember how much you loved him when he most needed a mom."

Capri nodded. "And how about we start a little journal? You can write letters to Lucan, and he can read them when he's old enough. It'll be like a bridge between your hearts until then."

Reva looked up, her eyes meeting those of her friends. A

flicker of hope, dim but undeniably present, lit up her gaze. She nodded, the ghost of a smile touching her lips. She sniffled again. "That sounds—really nice, actually. Thank you, all of you. As usual, I don't know what I'd do without you.

Aunt Mo, who had been sitting silently on the sofa, jumped up from her spot. "Horse manure!"

They all turned to face the older woman, their eyes wide.

"I say horse manure," she repeated.

"You are all forgetting there's someone in charge here...and it ain't us, and it ain't social services, and it most certainly ain't that man in prison who suddenly sees this little boy as his opportunity for early freedom." She pointed her finger straight up in the air. "From where I'm sitting, you girls have relinquished the situation and not asked the man upstairs for help." Her finger dropped and pointed to the lot of them. "You all might remember to talk to Him about this—and do it pretty soon. Time is running out."

The women immediately took her wise words to heart. They leaned in, forming a tight circle around Reva, their support palpable. Outside, the world continued to move, but inside, in the sanctuary of Reva's living room, time seemed to stand still as they rallied around one of their own.

And they prayed.

32

Reva stood at Kellen's front door, mustering all the resolve she could find. What she really wanted was to climb in bed and remain there hoping all this would pass over quickly, that she'd wake and find this situation was only a bad dream.

She took a deep breath and knocked. The door immediately opened.

"Reva. There you are. I've been worried." He motioned her inside.

"I'm so sorry. I know I haven't returned your calls and texts but..." Despite her resolve, tears bloomed.

"Reva?" Kellen's expression filled with concern. "What's the matter?"

Inside, the room was softly lit, creating an intimate atmosphere. Reva and Kellen sat close on the sofa, a half-finished glass of cola on the coffee table. Kellen looked at her with unwavering attention.

Reva took a deep breath. "Kellen, I'm sorry I didn't call and tell you earlier. It's about Lucan. He's...he's not with me right now. I had to leave him at social services."

Kellen's expression shifted from surprise to immediate concern. He reached for her hand, squeezing it gently. "Why? What happened?"

She solemnly explained the situation. Several times she had to pause and collect herself to keep from breaking down.

"Oh, Reva. I can't even begin to imagine how hard that must have been for you. What can I do?"

Reva's voice trembled. "I don't even know."

Kellen sat back, his gears clearly turning. After a moment, his resolve was apparent. "Well, I think I know."

KELLEN WALKED BRISKLY through the terminal, a determined look on his face. He was on a mission, his bag slung over his shoulder, heading towards his gate. When his flight was called, he handed over his boarding ticket to the attendant, granting her the obligatory smile, and then he headed down the breezeway. Minutes later, he was seated, buckled in, and headed for his destination.

The following morning, he woke bright and early and called a cab.

As Kellen slid into the taxi, he leaned against the seat of the musty sedan smelling of fast food and air freshener.

"Where you headin'?" the driver asked.

Kellen handed the driver a piece of paper with the address —a location that elicited a puzzled look from the old man behind the driver's wheel.

The seat, upholstered in once vibrant but now faded and slightly worn fabric, hinted at the cab's years of service. In the front, the dashboard was adorned with an array of personal mementos and trinkets belonging to the driver, including family photos wedged between the speedometer and the fuel gauge, and a small, bobbing-head dog positioned on the rearview mirror.

"Going to visit family?" the nosy driver asked.

"No," came Kellen's reply. "Just a...friend."

Okay, that was a little white lie. But the situation warranted a white lie and more.

As the cab wove through the city streets, the soft buzz of the radio played in the background, the driver occasionally humming along to a familiar tune. The back seat offered a confined space, just enough for Kellen to stretch his legs slightly before they bumped against the seat in front at the next curve. Every turn and stop brought a chorus of creaks and groans from the vehicle, telling the tale of its many journeys.

Looking out of the slightly tinted windows, Kellen watched the world blur by, the rhythmic motion of the cab almost soothing. Despite the cab's humble and worn interior, there was a sense of life and stories within its confines, a silent witness to the countless individuals it had transported. As they approached the prison, the realization of their destination cast a somber shadow over the journey, turning Kellen's attention away from the cab to thoughts of what awaited him at the end of the ride.

What he had in mind was a win-or-lose proposition. The stakes were high.

He only hoped that the scales would tip in the right direction and this one would land in the win column.

33

Kellen reached the front entry door and stepped into the large, old brick building and out of the baking Texas sun, the inside air a welcome respite from the heat emanating from the concrete. Despite the cooler temperature, sweat formed on his scalp.

A woman officer dressed in a blue shirt, damp at the underarms, stepped forward. "I'll need your driver's license." She thrust a clipboard at Kellen. "Sign at the designated spot and put the time next to your name." She tilted her head toward a large clock on the opposite wall. "And place your belongings in the basket."

He swallowed and did as he was told. When finished, he held up the basket to the officer.

The woman pointed to a wall lined with lockers and handed him a key. "Over there."

As soon as Kellen stored his belongings, he glanced around, confused about where to go next. An older black lady with white hair gave him a toothy smile and pointed toward a metal door with a sign posted above that read "Visitors Holding Room."

Kellen gave the lady a token nod of gratitude and followed a crowd of people moving in that direction. After passing through the metal detector, he was patted down by another female officer, who smelled of cigarettes and maple syrup. "Wait over there," the woman said, pointing to metal chairs lined up against a pea-green wall in bad need of paint.

He nodded and scanned for an empty chair, then sat to wait.

A man moved past, mopping the floor. His shoes made a slight squeaky sound every time he sludged forward, slowly pulling the dirty-looking mop across the speckled linoleum floor.

Kellen leaned his head back against the cold, hard wall of the holding room, keeping his eyes closed so he wouldn't have to see countless young girls waiting to see their baby daddies. The sight was far too depressing.

"Kellen Warner?"

The booming voice caused him to startle. He glanced about the room. "Me?" he asked.

The officer with the clipboard heaved a sigh laced with boredom. "Your name Warner?"

Kellen nodded and stood. He followed the officer through the door and down a long hallway with windowless walls the color of dried mud.

He was led through a heavy metal door into a room less than half the size of his tiny kitchen at home. A barrier cut the room in half, the upper portion made of glass grimy with hand-prints. The scene was straight out of a television episode of *CSI*.

Kellen turned to thank the officer, but he was now alone. Nervous, he slid into the empty chair on his side of the barrier.

And waited.

Then Jess Dorsey entered, appearing older, more tired than the photos Kellen had found on the internet.

Lucan's grandfather quickly moved to the window and took

his seat. With a guard standing nearby, he placed his shackled palm against the glass and mouthed, “Do I know you?”

Kellen blinked several times before picking up the telephone receiver and motioning for him to do the same.

The older black man who was graying at the temples scrambled for the phone at his side and nestled the black handset against his ear. “What do you want?” he asked, his voice gruff and impatient.

Over the next minutes, Kellen told him exactly why he was here and what he wanted.

34

Reva found herself settled in the heart of her living room, encircled by her dearest friends and neighbors.

In the kitchen, Charlie Grace busied herself with arranging a sandwich platter, while Lila gently stirred a pitcher of lemonade. Capri took charge of filling the ice bucket.

Nearby, Nicola and Wooster Cavendish stood by the window, close to Albie, as Gibbs and Lizzy cozied up on a blanket, cradling their newborn.

The Knit Wit ladies, perched on folding chairs, engaged in eager speculation, buzzing with curiosity about the purpose of their gathering. Even Pete and Annie Cumberland had joined, pausing their duties at the Rustic Pine for the afternoon to be there.

A palpable sense of expectation filled the air, a collective sense of being on the cusp of learning something significant—yet none of them were privy to the details.

Kellen cleared his throat, drawing the attention of everyone in the room. His eyes met Reva's, a spark of nervous excitement flickering in his gaze. "I have something to share," he began, his voice steady yet filled with emotion. "Something I did, hoping it would bring us all closer to a resolution we've been dreaming of."

Reva leaned forward, her heart beating a little faster, knowing that whatever Kellen was about to reveal, it was important.

"I went to see Lucan's grandfather in prison," Kellen continued, his admission hanging in the air. The room fell silent, the weight of his words settling over them like a blanket. Reva's eyes widened in surprise, and she instinctively glanced at the crowd, who seemed as astonished as she at this news.

"I'm not sure I'm following you, Kellen," she said, her hands slightly trembling.

Kellen recounted his visit, detailing the conversation with Lucan's grandfather, the heartfelt plea for a new beginning, and the discussion of the hard truths about the challenges facing young black men without guidance. "I told him about the love and stability this community can offer Lucan," he said, his voice thick with emotion. He moved to join Reva and placed his arm around her waist. "And about the future we could build together, as a family."

"What are you talking about?" Capri demanded. "You went to see that guy in jail?"

Kellen nodded. "I offered him a recommendation for release and a job when he got out, with me at Warner Automotive. I also offered him a place to live and an opportunity for a supervised internship where he can learn new skills and support himself. A fresh start. A start near his grandson."

Reva's lip quivered as she drew an unstable breath. "What are you saying, Kellen?"

He turned and took her hands in his, brought them to his mouth, and kissed her knuckles. "I'm saying he agreed to an open adoption—with the provision he remains as Lucan's official grandfather with full visitation. And Lucan is to retain the surname Dorsey."

Kellen looked at Reva, who was now shaking with emotion. "I thought you'd agree to those terms."

As Kellen spoke of the tear that had slipped down the old man's cheek, a sign of his understanding and acceptance of the proposed offer, Reva felt her own eyes well up with tears. The grandfather had agreed to put Lucan's well-being above all else after all.

There was a knock on the door. Jewel scrambled over and threw it open.

Bea Followill stood there with Lucan in her arms. "I believe I have something of yours," she offered, her face brimming with delight.

The room erupted into a mixture of shocked gasps and soft cries of joy. Reva reached for Lucan, her hands shaking as she took his little body and pulled him against her, a gesture filled with gratitude and love. "Ma-ma?" he gurgled with a wide grin.

Incredulous, her voice a mere whisper, she asked Kellen, "You did this for us? For Lucan?"

A smile pierced Kellen's usually somber expression. He nodded. "For all of us, for the family we might someday become."

The realization of what Kellen's words and actions meant—for Lucan's future and hers—swept through the room. Sensing the shift in emotions, Lucan abandoned the toy he was holding. He climbed from Reva's embrace into Kellen's arms, looking from face to face with curious eyes.

"We're going to be a real family, Lucan," Reva whispered to him, her voice steady despite the tears streaming down her cheeks. "You're going to grow up surrounded by so much love, and your grandfather...he's going to be part of our lives too."

As she and Kellen gathered closer, the boundaries between them blurred, united by a profound sense of family and a future filled with hope. While their relationship was new and uncharted, there was little doubt they were embarking on a journey together, fortified by the love and sacrifices that had led them to this moment—a moment born from Kellen's courage and compassion that had marked the dawn of a new chapter for them all.

Reva looked around the room at these people who were so dear to her. She glanced at Kellen holding Lucan. Big crocodile tears of happiness and pure joy rolled down her cheeks. These were the moments that would echo in her heart forever.

She simply couldn't ask for more.

AUTHOR'S NOTE

Dear Readers,

Thank you from the bottom of my heart for reading and embracing "Echoes of the Heart" along with the entire Teton Mountain Series. These stories are a tribute to the enduring power of friendship, a theme close to my heart. I'm endlessly thankful for the deep bonds I share with my lifelong friends and those I've met along the way; their support has been a blessing beyond what can be described with mere words.

"Echoes of the Heart" also delves into a theme that resonated deeply with me during a World Orphan's Day service at my local church. It was there that a fellow member shared her family's heart-touching journey. Lesli Thompson and her husband, Jeff, have opened their hearts and home as foster parents to infants in need within the Dallas/Fort Worth community. Lesli's words struck a chord with me:

"Orphans are easier to ignore before you know their names.

They are easier to ignore before you see their faces. It is easier to pretend they're not real before you hold them in your arms, but once you do...everything changes."

Hearing Lesli recount her experiences, including the profound sadness of returning a child to his biological family after caring for him for over a year, followed by the distress of caring for an abused baby who had suffered broken arms and legs at the age of seven weeks, was a pivotal moment for me. It underscored the staggering reality faced by children in the foster care system—153 million worldwide, including 390,000 in the United States. Lesli's plea to our congregation was a call to action: to open our homes, offer support to foster families, or financially contribute to local agencies making a difference in these children's lives. Her message was clear: "We only have one life to live...one life to be the agent of change."

This experience compelled me to write Reva's story in "Echoes of the Heart." While my narratives steer clear of darkness, I aimed to evoke deep emotional engagement with Reva's journey, exploring her bond with Lucan and the heartache of potentially letting him go. Writing offers me the solace of crafting a hopeful conclusion, a "happily ever after" that life often withholds. Be assured, Echoes of the Heart leaves readers feeling joy.

I invite you to keep these children and the courageous individuals like Lesli and Jeff in your prayers. They venture beyond their comfort zones to make a meaningful difference in the lives of children who are often at their most vulnerable.

For those interested in hearing Lesli's full presentation, I encourage you to do so. You can find a link to the YouTube video on my website. It's a moving account that will likely require some tissues.

With gratitude,

Kellie Coates Gilbert

ABOUT THE AUTHOR

USA Today Bestselling Author Kellie Coates Gilbert has won readers' hearts with her heartwarming and highly emotional stories about women and the relationships that define their lives. As a former legal investigator, Kellie brings a unique blend of insight and authenticity to her stories, ensuring that readers are hooked from the very first page.

In addition to garnering hundreds of five-star reviews, Kellie has been described by RT Book Reviews as a "deft, crisp storyteller." Her books were featured as Barnes & Noble Top Shelf Picks and earned a coveted place on Library Journal's Best Book List.

Kellie now lives with her husband of over thirty-five years in

Dallas, where she spends most days by her pool drinking sweet tea and writing the stories of her heart.

Ready to read more Kellie Coates Gilbert books? Be sure to check out my store where you can get exclusive deals:

www.kelliecoatesgilbertbooks.com

You can also find links to other retailers on my website:

www.kelliecoatesgilbert.com/books

Join my private Facebook reader group *GILBERT GIRLS* where I chat every day, do fun giveaways and live broadcasts, and offer special opportunities to read new releases early:

www.facebook.com/groups/gilbertgirlsreadergroup

Want to get my newsletters where I share upcoming releases and discounts? Sign up at my website:

www.kelliecoatesgilbert.com

-

-

Reviews help other readers find new books, including mine. I always appreciate it when my readers take the time to leave an honest review.

I love to hear from my readers. Feel free to contact me at kellie@kelliecoatesgilbert.com

ALSO BY KELLIE COATES GILBERT

Thank you for reading this story. If you'd like to read more of my books, please check out these series. To purchase at special discounts: www.kelliecoatesgilbertbooks.com

TETON MOUNTAIN SERIES

Where We Belong – Book 1

Echoes of the Heart – Book 2

Holding the Dream – Book 3

As the Sun Rises – Book 4

MAUI ISLAND SERIES

Under the Maui Sky – Book 1

Silver Island Moon – Book 2

Tides of Paradise – Book 3

The Last Aloha – Book 4

Ohana Sunrise – Book 5

Sweet Plumeria Dawn – Book 6

Songs of the Rainbow – Book 7

Hibiscus Christmas – Book 8

PACIFIC BAY SERIES

Chances Are – Book 1

Remember Us – Book 2

Chasing Wind – Book 3

Between Rains – Book 4

SUN VALLEY SERIES

Sisters – Book 1

Heartbeats – Book 2

Changes – Book 3

Promises – Book 4

TEXAS GOLD COLLECTION

A Woman of Fortune – Book 1

Where Rivers Part – Book 2

A Reason to Stay – Book 3

What Matters Most – Book 4

STAND ALONE NOVELS:

Mother of Pearl

AVAILABLE AT ALL MAJOR RETAILERS

FOR EXCLUSIVE DISCOUNTS:

www.kelliecoatesgilbertbooks.com

Made in the USA
Las Vegas, NV
16 January 2025

16508176R00125